# A WAVE IN TIME

# A WAVE IN TIME

MIKE BRITTON

Printed in the United States of America

ISBN: 979-8-9947441-0-9

*To a forever friend, Bill Lee,*
*who was lost to this world too early.*

*I fear the day that technology will surpass our human interaction. The world will have a generation of idiots.*

—Albert Einstein

# PROLOGUE

## Wednesday, June 15, 2050

After ten years of propagating through the cosmos, a gravitational wave, born in the cold, dark depths of space, approaches the outer limits of our solar system's heliosphere. It passes through space dust, asteroids, and comets. In the distance, the Sun appears and, just beyond, a small blue dot. The dot gets bigger and bigger: Earth. Then, in less than the time it takes for a human to blink, the wave passes through Earth and changes the trajectory of life on our planet forever.

# 1

# THE ARCHITECT

### Sixteen Days Earlier

Unaware of the approaching gravitational wave, the Architect sits alone in a shadowy corner of the conference room, quietly contemplating the dichotomy of today's meeting before the others arrive. The stated goals are to promote the platform's new enhancements and to coerce the remaining holdouts to become hosts. However, for the Architect, this is merely a preliminary step toward a larger plan to initiate the Path Program and save Earth for centuries to come. The Architect never speaks such things aloud, even in a whisper. These thoughts are far too confidential for most who will soon gather. As this secret lingers in the dark corner of the Architect's mind, the soft hum of arial vehicles can be heard.

Outside, in the shadow of the jagged Idaho Mountains, a select circle of the world's most powerful figures arrive one by one. Their private shuttles touch down in one clearing after another, their rotors stirring up clouds of dust and scattering startled sparrows into the crisp Idaho sky. The majestic beauty of the mountains, the sweet scent of sun-warmed pine needles, and the gentle rhythm of the streams provide a peaceful background as leaders from the pinnacles of global business, military command, and political power gather for a reckoning that will shape the fate of untold billions. Each carries a slim obsidian card, personalized and valid for this day only, May 30, 2050.

Yet for all the serenity outside, tension mounts within the group as they step through the camouflaged entrance to the mountain's interior. The cavernous halls are filled with the thrum of filtered air and the faint tang of minerals. Inside the conference room, however, the air is thick with anticipation, the weight of the moment pressing down as steel doors lock in place behind them.

A tall, severe man, the Chairman has always commanded these meetings easily, and when he calls the meeting to order, silence falls at once. His ice-blue gaze misses nothing, part of his sharp senses refined from his former career as a general whose legacy was built on ruthless efficiency in a crisis.

"Ladies and gentlemen, I recognize the demands on your time," the Chairman begins. "However, this gathering is imperative, as we're determining the future direction of life on our planet. As leaders of your respective zones, it's critical you listen carefully and execute these final instructions with perfection. Any leaks or deviations from the plan will have deadly consequences."

While others in the room shout their questions, the

Architect quietly doodles in a notebook. The pencil wanders the page, sketching a mountain range like the one outside. Though not one for morbid reflection, the Architect wonders at the fragility of human existence, at the tidal changes that have occurred within one lifetime, and who is at fault. Not long ago, people still had regular jobs: machinist, copywriter, surgeon. But in the matter of a generation, things started to change, slowly at first and then all at once. Artificial superintelligence forced the masses to redefine who they were and how to derive value in a world where most essential products and services are provided by the government. Adults in every developed country were forced out of work, including the Architect's father, whose large personality contracted in real time, until he was as blank and stolid as the machines that delivered groceries and medicine to their home on an allotted schedule.

Although the Architect sympathized with the plight of family and the population at first, over time, frustrations grew. Productivity was exploding...it was all over the news! How could the billions not see that this new reality was better? And so, the Architect's destiny became entangled into the mainframe of the future. There was no doubt in the Architect's mind that, without the gift of the platform, the masses would drift like a rudderless boat on the ocean and become restless, or worse. To keep it all from falling apart, the platform became the best gift the people of this world had ever received.

The Chairman asks for a show of hands to signal their agreement with the latest proposal. On cue, extended right arms fill the room, except for one.

*Who is at fault?* ponders the Architect. *They needed salvation, making them complicit in their own demise. We now must do what is best for the planet, as the current path is unsustainable. The world needs relief, and the masses need to find hope again. Of course, our plans require sacrifice, but in doing so, it ensures our survival.*

Another participant shakes the Architect's shoulder. "Aren't you listening? You missed the vote, and now the Chairman has asked you twice for an update on the resistance forces and timing for our stem cell treatments."

The Architect snaps from the daydream, face slick with sweat. One final thought forms before speaking. *We will do so much good with just one single act. In a couple weeks, it will all be over as the Path Program reshapes the world. Nothing can stop us now!*

# 2

# GLOBAL OPERATION AND DESIGN

Located north of Los Angeles, the headquarters of Global Operation and Design (GOD) is a massive, military-inspired complex. GOD is the center of economic and political power and the world's largest monopoly. Its public mission is to advance human interests through technological innovation across all scientific and humanitarian fields. For over twenty years, GOD has successfully achieved its objectives while quietly manipulating the minds of its nine billion hosts through a hyper-addictive lifestyle platform called Augmented Individualism, or the AIP.

Uniformed security personnel, canines, and aerial drones patrol GOD's premises, which have been designed with complexities reminiscent of a labyrinthine corn maze. From a bird's-eye view, it's easy to see how to navigate, but on the ground, the pine trees, bushes, fake walls, and retention ponds will disorient anyone unfamiliar with the layout.

Two guards approach each other from opposite directions.

"Anything look suspicious this time around?" guard one asks.

"Are you kidding? This place is locked down tighter than Fort Knox."

"Not sure why they have us humans making the rounds with all the other security protocols in place. There's no chance I would sense something wrong before Rover here." Guard one looks down at his canine companion, a Labrador-shaped robot embedded with sensors to detect unusual sounds, motion, or any type of chemicals in the air...all covered by a fake, black fur coat.

The second guard adds, "And our eye in the sky never sleeps," as a drone eagle glides over their heads with a woosh.

"This is a civilian facility. I can't imagine what security must be like around one of the government locations."

Both men laugh as they separate and descend back into the darkness of the trees.

An autonomous cargo truck arrives at GOD's back security gate, moves onto a conveyor belt, and enters a small building. Reminiscent of an old hands-free car wash, the cargo truck proceeds through a sequence of scanning devices and chemical sensors for inspection. Near the end, a logistics humanoid accesses the security manifest to verify the authorized weight of the cargo truck. The scale reads 125,223 pounds; twenty pounds heavier than the manifest record. A series of high-pitched sirens pierce the air, causing a dozen armed security humanoids to activate. They burst from concealed locations to take strategic positions around the vehicle.

A voice comes over the loudspeaker. "H4 and H8, go in for a closer inspection." The two humanoids approach the cargo truck and make an initial ground-level visual inspection. The voice gives further instructions: "H8, enter the cargo hold. H4, climb the back ladder and inspect the roof." Moments later, a raccoon is thrown from the roof and scampers out of the building. H4 climbs back down and moves away from the cargo truck. The scale in the background reads 125,202 pounds. The voice says, "Close enough. Send it to the receiving dock." The security humanoids fade back into the shadows and deactivate.

The receiving dock is busy with crews processing palletized containers. Humans perform quality-control testing while the loading humanoids move materials into the facility. "Hey, Sarge, how long are we supposed to keep pulling double time?" one of the dock workers asks.

"Haven't got a clue. Orders come from the top, and we do what we're told. Any complaints and there won't be any jobs left for us." He turns, glaring at the closest humanoid.

Descending belowground, GOD's sheer scale, level of security, and use of technology is overwhelming. An interconnected series of three-directional moving sidewalks and elevators efficiently move thousands of employees to their required locations. Background noise is piped throughout the structure to discourage idle chatter and the possibility of sharing confidential information. Scanners register entry and exit locations based on security clearance. The quantum-control systems know exactly where everyone needs to be, and no one goes outside of preapproved locations unnoticed.

The brain center of the facility is located below ground in the innermost center of the headquarters. Scented air-scrubbing systems and UV-light replicators shine through digital window casings while physiological audio interceptors are at work helping to mitigate any feelings of claustrophobia. The moving walkway transitions into a short, sterile concrete tunnel with a "Quantum Solutions" sign above the large metal doorway at the end. A man places his hand on a pad to the right of the doorway, prompting an iris scanner to activate. A few seconds later, he enters into a washed-out, off-white hallway as the door closes tightly behind him. Einstein's quote "God Does Not Play Dice" greets every person upon arrival as a reminder to execute their jobs to perfection.

# 3

## THE ENGINEER

Inside GOD's quantum-solutions control room, a team of human engineers are working, seamlessly moving between scores of computer tables with three-dimensional outputs. Each table hosts a uniquely skilled artificial intelligence program. The engineers have been chosen based on stringent criteria, and together with their artificial intelligence counterparts, they form the most capable quantum systems hardware and software team globally.

Individual team members work and move as if there's no coordination between their actions, but a rhythm develops. One team member finishes an action and sends the output screen to another team member. This pattern continues uninterrupted, until one member, named Kendra, says, "The bug has been identified, and exterminated."

Holding an empty can of bug spray, she motions to the back of the room and says, "Hey, Matt, that insect just entered a no-fly zone."

The team responds affirmatively. One member holds up a card with a 9.5 score, while two other team members exchange an air high five. However, everyone's primary interest lies in receiving feedback from Matt.

Kendra turns toward the far corner office and yells, "Right, Matt?"

The man does not answer, doesn't respond in any way, his full focus on the multidimensional system diagrams in front of him. Matt Boson is the executive design engineer for all quantum systems at GOD. Always deeply ensconced in his work, he's regularly mocked by his team for his fastidious dedication.

One of the engineers yells out, "Hey, Kendra. Are you sure he's here? It's awfully quiet back there."

She replies, "Oh yeah. I see a head with short, blond hair, a six-foot-something frame, and some muscles tucked neatly behind a figure that has added several pounds these last couple years. There's also the wrinkled blue sweatshirt, the same one we saw him wearing yesterday and the day before that. And if that's not enough, I can see his eyes!"

Matt hears everything, grins ever so slightly, and stands up. His one green eye and one brown eye shimmer in the unnatural office light. His condition is called heterochromia and is very rare. "Until the eye thing, it could have been anyone back here," he jokes.

"Come on, live a little," is yelled from the front of the room.

Matt smirks and turns back to his screen.

A manager named Eugene steps in. "Leave him alone. He's one of us...only from a different level. The top brass doesn't cut him a break, so let's not pile on from our end also. We all know there's no better boss in the whole company."

Matt comments, "Thanks, Eugene, but the team is right. I need to get out of my own head, get out of the code, get out of the game every now and then to live my life. I'm sorry it's so unnatural to me. I should be making sure you feel appreciated for all the great work we've done together. I may get credit from the suits on the upper floors, but without your dedication and unique knowledge, there would be none to give."

"Hey, boss, skip the speech. We know the 'superposition' we're in and how you feel." Laughter erupts at the quantum double entendre. "What we want is to say goodnight to all these qubits and go out for a drink at our usual watering hole. No rank, no judgment, and 'no' is not an answer."

Matt's out the door before anyone realizes it, his voice trailing down the hall. "What time are you planning to be there?"

Eugene responds, "Any time you want, boss," and then feels a glare burning his back.

Kendra says, "You know without being very specific with him, he won't show."

Without turning to face the team, Eugene exclaims, "He said he'd be there."

"Yeah, but he didn't even ask where we were going."

Matt exits GOD's main building and waits in a short queue for an autonomous taxi ride home. He enters the vehicle, places his hand on the passenger-seat scanner, and says, "Home please."

It's a drive he's made a thousand times, starting in the secluded area near the headquarters building and quickly changing to the low-rise clutter of the city's outskirt population. Shortly after, the mid-rise neighborhoods start, easily recognizable by both the change in restaurant quality and the building heights.

Matt exits the taxi and climbs his building's steps to the security door. The body scanner verifies his biometric data and unlocks his front door; a familiar feeling of guilt comes over him. *Why do you do this, leading them on when you know you're not going back out?*

Matt's condominium betrays the fact he's a minimalist. Its contents are extremely sparse but meticulously clean and organized. A vacuum remains available to clean up anything that may have been missed by the robotic housekeeping service. He changes into his pajamas and notices the hair clippers on the counter in the bathroom. *I can't believe I forgot to put those away this morning. I must be slipping.*

Making the short walk to the kitchen, he opens the refrigerator, looks at the top two shelves of drinks arranged alphabetically, and grabs a beer from the first shelf. Moving down the fridge to the premade meals, he takes the container labeled "Tuesday's dinner" and places it in the electrodynamic heater.

*Is it one minute and eight seconds or one minute and eighteen seconds for the proper temperature?* After several moments standing motionless, eyes focused straight ahead as if there were an instructional cooking diagram floating in front of the kitchen cabinets, he gives the voice command: "One minute and eight seconds." *Mental note: add the cooking time on my labels to avoid unneeded indecision.*

Matt cracks his beer and walks through the dining area toward the living room, his head awkwardly positioned to look at the ceiling as he takes a long drink. Plopping on the floor, he places the empty beer can on a side table and stares out the window. Moments later, the ding of his warm meal snaps him out of it. *Oh crap, back I go.* He cocks his head again to avoid the police reports and newspaper articles spread across the dining room table. *It's been twenty years since my father disappeared, and it's still too raw for me to read them or put them away.*

After finishing dinner, he looks deep into the nighttime stars, trying to justify his decision to stay in. *Nothing makes you weaker than a non-predictable wave equation, except perhaps too many cocktails. Good decision.*

On the outskirts of town, Eugene stares at a bottle of beer on the other side of the table.

One of his colleagues says, "That beer looks lonelier than you do sitting by yourself. It's been over two hours, and he isn't coming. It's time to pay up."

Eugene sends the digital payment, grabs the beer, and chugs it back. "I guess you were right...again."

His colleagues confirm receipt of the wager. "When will you ever learn? Matt can't be one of us."

# 4

# THE ASTROPHYSICIST

Like clockwork, the sky transitions from gray to blue as the sun burns off the overnight ocean moisture. Students move quickly in all directions as the new semester's classes are about to start.

Despite opening only ten years ago, the campus carries a dense smell of privilege. A first-year student pauses in front of the central-square monument for a selfie. A Princeton West Coast plaque is visible on all four sides. The campus architectural designs are carefully crafted to reflect an East Coast Ivy League school, that is, for all buildings except one.

The Advanced Physics Center was funded by a grant from Global Operations and Design. The only string attached: GOD's engineering resources construct the building following tight specifications from GOD. The three-story building is smooth and symmetrical except for a series of concave carveouts, one at each corner of the three floors and one encasing the main entrance to the building.

Each carveout displays a tribute to a great physicist, with the main entrance reserved for the greatest of them all.

The building's interior is meticulously designed to foster intellectual growth. Inside one state-of-the-art teaching room, students move quietly around a three-dimensional blackboard displaying cosmological events from various reference points.

The professor, Alyssa Starr, is teaching an entry-level class on astrophysics. Despite the age difference, Alyssa has a youthful look and wears designer clothes that make it hard to distinguish her from the students. Even in her forties, she doesn't need to wear makeup, a fact muttered every semester under the breath of varying groups of jealous female students.

Alyssa's coffee-brown eyes and straight, dark hair complement her porcelain skin. The only noticeable imperfection is a distinctive lightning-shaped, natural-gray streak of hair on her left side, which caused her embarrassment as a child. Her parents would tell her it symbolized her high energy level.

Aware that her tall, lean stature would block the view of most of the class, she stands behind the encircling group as she says, "Supermassive gravitational bodies like this galaxy cluster bend the passing light waves from the quasar behind it, creating what we observe as an Einstein ring." Her voice carries an air of privilege, not unlike the students, who shuffle back and forth to take in the full effect.

One student asks, "Why should Einstein get credit for this?"

Alyssa states, "His general theory of relativity predicted

their existence long before they were observed. Isn't it fitting to name it after him now that we have so many examples to prove he was right?"

"He must have been a smart dude. His name is above the main entrance doors."

Alyssa plays along, knowing full well the students are aware of his significance to the school. "Yes, he was a smart dude. So smart, in fact, he taught at Princeton in the 1930s, and we know only the best and brightest teach at Princeton." She takes a bow and smiles as a light medley of clapping fills the room.

She continues. "In all seriousness, scientists often predict various cosmic phenomena before they're able to confirm them. Let's take gravitational waves as an example. Predicted as far back as 1893, they're short-term displacements in a gravitational field, generated by the relative motion or disturbance of a gravitational mass. They're exceedingly difficult to measure, and even with our recent technological advancements, we struggle to 'see' any significant waves."

A student asks, "What type of disturbance would cause a significant wave?"

Alyssa replies, "Well, um...like a collision between two objects much more massive than anything in our solar system."

"Even the sun?" the student asks.

"Correct. Even as large as our Sun is, it's not massive enough."

"What would happen if there were a relevant event?"

Alyssa is in her element. "Gravitational waves radiate outward from their source at the speed of light. In the general theory of relativity, gravitational waves manifest as ripples in space-time. It's a difficult concept, but think of throwing a rock into a pond of still water. As the rock hits the water, it creates a disturbance, which we observe as concentric circles of waves. The waves carry energy away from where the rock hits the water. It's no different with a gravitational wave except the disturbance is with space-time, causing space and time to shrink and expand as the gravitational wave passes through."

"So we don't have many of them here on Earth?" a student blurts out.

"In fact, yes, gravitational waves are passing through us right now. It's just that there are no significant gravitational disturbances close enough to Earth for this to be an issue to anyone here in the classroom. Only at the smallest quantum levels would there ever be a recognition of the waves."

A student asks, "Have you ever been to space yourself?"

"No, my work has been solely terrestrial."

"But surely you must have had the option. Isn't your husband the CEO for the Daedalus Space Exploration Company, and aren't you independently wealthy?"

"First, ex-husband, and second, none of your business." Several students wince. "I didn't need to go into space to study it. After all, you don't need to travel to the southern border to know where Mexico is or inoculate yourself with Ebola to examine it. Do you?"

The bell rings and the three-dimensional blackboard goes dark. Alyssa reminds the class, "Next time, we'll discuss a more difficult topic, quantum entanglement."

"Can't wait, good times," says a student.

Alyssa receives a high five as the class empties into the hallway. Her thoughts drift to her company's recent launch of its advanced satellite array. *The combination of satellite-based gravitational wave detectors and placement of these satellites beyond the Sun will give us a unique view outside our solar system. The first observational data should be coming in soon, but I don't expect to solve any mysteries today. We'll start with observations from an innocuous hydrogen gas cloud to give the artificial intelligence software an easy assignment out of the blocks.*

She smiles as the next group of students file in.

# 5

## THE FARMHOUSE

An oak-lined driveway forms a straight line toward the Johnson farmhouse, built generations ago to be resilient to the hazards of nature that come with living in the nation's Midwest. The closest oak to the house supports a rope swing that the Johnsons haven't used in a generation. A full wraparound porch, once the stage for large social gatherings, is in grave danger of being crushed by several large branches. A light-blue tarp covers the south end of the roof, evidence of the ferocity of a past thunderstorm.

Looking out from the farmhouse, there are genetically modified crops covering the ground as far as the eye can see. The only other structure is a well-maintained barn used to store the autonomous equipment for each year's planting and harvest.

Today, there is only one surviving Johnson family member living in the house. As urban farmers, his ancestors labored to plant, manage, and harvest the fields as he did for the first fifty years of his life. It was a time when all parts of nature worked together in harmony with the farmer in the middle. Many times, he has longed for days of the past. But now, after years of marginalization, he carries a sense of helplessness.

Each season now, autonomous machinery supported by robotic labor does everything, leaving him with a sense of uselessness and despair. If not for a meaningless part-time job and the pleasureful experiences of his digital avatar, it would be hard to fight off the impulse to end his own life or join a revolt.

In a dimly lit room, the farmer finishes his dinner and carefully stacks his warm plate on top of similar cold ones from the past few days. *I'll get to those soon.* He sits motionless with his eyes closed. Vivid scenes flash across the insides of his eyelids. His heart rate and breathing increase in anticipation of his avatar's evening entertainment. The farmer's eyes open, pupils dilated, the excitement too much to delay any longer as he reaches for his augmented reality connector (ARC).

Revolutionary advancements in quantum learning enable neurostimulators inside the ARC to replicate a host's senses. GOD provides the ARC and access to the AIP for free in exchange for a simple acceptance of its "terms and conditions."

The farmer's ARC engages, hijacking all neural connections to his brain. He's now living in the digital world, feeling, seeing, hearing, tasting, and smelling whatever his avatar is engaged in. The farmer doesn't hear the watering protocol start outside. He's more interested in assuring he secures a happy ending from the date his avatar is starting.

# 6

## THE CEO

The penthouse suite at GOD headquarters houses the office of its CEO, Niera Kristain. Its ten-thousand-square-foot floor plan is simple: an executive office, two conference rooms, an overnight residence for nights when returning home is impractical, and a series of back passageways accessible only to Niera.

It's 8:00 a.m., and the last bits of steam dissipate out of the white Italian-marble executive shower. A female figure stands in front of the mirror, shoulders pulled back, the outline of her abs evident through her blouse. She smiles and thinks, *Tight figure, no wrinkles despite years of battle, sparkling-white teeth, brown eyes to complement perfectly placed blonde highlights. You look good enough at fifty-five to go toe-to-toe with any of the thirty-somethings in the office.*

Niera Kristain has done well in her life, and her office is a shrine to that fact. Several plaques for individual achievements and corporate innovation awards are showcased alongside framed photographs of her with distinguished public and governmental leaders. A careful inspection of the pictures shows the individuals to be in awe of standing alongside Niera.

For more than twenty years, Niera has held the CEO title. In many ways, her job is much like that of any other CEO of a global monopoly. There are macro supply chain and geopolitical challenges along with micro personnel and finance issues to deal with. Today, she wants an update on a particularly persistent network of hackers and on her company's progress in moving more of its server facilities within city boundaries, where humanoid policing resources can more efficiently identify and squash any physical threats to the facilities.

Niera's assistant, Jacob, pushes open her private office door to see a familiar sight: Niera transfixed, staring into the mirror. He waits a few seconds, debating whether to be honest about her clothes not fitting as well as they did years ago. He concludes it's not worth the risk and says, "Time to go, Niera. We can't keep your team waiting any longer."

Niera enters the conference room through a private back door: her steely eyes canvas the room, taking into account who is sitting and who is standing. *Pretty much as I expected, those public relations people are always nervous, never seeming able to sit and relax, especially when their boss is on vacation. I'm a little surprised Tom from legal is standing in the corner.*

Niera takes a seat at the head of the table. "Shall we get started? Who wants to go first with updates?"

Without waiting for a volunteer, she glances over her right shoulder at the public relations team and asks, "How well have you done keeping the recent hacking episodes out of the media?"

The three team members shuffle, knowing full well Niera already has the answer.

She waits five seconds...no response. Niera screams, "For God's sake, someone open your fucking mouth and tell me something I'm willing to accept as comforting."

The team's youngest member steps forward. "Uh, well, Ms. Kristain, we've been in constant contact with all the media outlets, and our pressure has been successful in getting them to sit back and say nothing, until this morning. The problem is, someone leaked details of the hacking in a public chat forum and now the media is saying they must release the story. You know...to protect their own integrity."

"So we've not contained the situation," Niera fires back.

"No, ma'am," she says, lowering her head to better prepare for the storm.

Niera leans forward to look at Tasha Watts, head of human resources. Before speaking, Niera extends her right arm, her defined muscles twitching as she locks her arm in place. Her index finger points like a deadly arrow at the head of purchasing, Mr. Campbell. Tiny blood vessels on the surface of Niera's eyes expand, turning the white into a reddish hue. She begins speaking directly at Tasha, knowing full well the impact it will have on the accused.

"Tasha, I want you to escort Mr. Campbell directly out

of the building. His personal effects are in a box outside this conference room door. Do not let him interact with anyone on the way out, and by the time he gets home, I want a breach-of-confidentiality lawsuit at his doorstep. And this next part is important. I want our delivery agent to verbally emphasize to him and his spouse just how screwed they are."

Tasha responds immediately, taking Mr. Campbell by the arm and moving him toward the door. The other PR team members follow, being careful not to step into the puddle their colleague just created.

Niera's breathing returns to normal as the redness in her eyes fades. She looks at the others in the room and continues. "It gives me minimal pleasure doing this, but our head of security, Fitz, uncovered the truth this morning and we need to exterminate the rats!"

Before moving on, she smiles at the man sitting to her left, Drazen Ram. Drazen is the COO for GOD. He's a few years younger than Niera and is considered her "favorite" among the other executive leaders.

He winks at Niera, a quick sign of approval for her actions.

Having received affirmation, Niera moves on to Matt Boson. "I approved your request for the new headcount. When do you expect to have the positions filled?"

"Already took care of it," Matt says with pride. "They start next week."

"Great. How are you planning to integrate them into your existing team? We have an especially important software upgrade coming, and we need all the horsepower we can get from your servers."

Matt's eyes narrow. He cocks his head and says, "I'm not sure I understand your reference. Horsepower is a mechanical derivative, and we use quantum uncertainty to solve our problems."

Niera laughs and replies, "This is why we all love you, Matt." She tips her head, her pupils expand, and the sound of laughter becomes a distant memory. "But you realize we've seen a dip in marginal server productivity month over month?"

"I'm looking into it."

Recognizing the cliff is approaching like an iceberg toward a cruise ship, Drazen steps in. "Why don't you let me deal with Matt on that issue? After all, he does report to me. And besides, you and I have bigger issues to discuss in private."

Niera nods in agreement.

Drazen leans over to Matt and whispers, "It's best for you to get out while you can. I'll check in later."

"Could not agree more. I hate coming to this conference room." Matt leaves without saying goodbye.

"That boy is in a world of his own," Niera comments.

"Yes, but he's the best in his field."

"Second best," replies Niera, returning the wink. "Now, let's keep moving so we can get our private time together."

Niera swivels her chair toward her chief legal officer, Tom, and asks, "Why are you hiding in the corner?"

"Not hiding, observing," Tom says.

"Whatever. We have one critical intellectual-property lawsuit still open. I need you to finish it or make it go away!"

"I can't wave a magic wand, Niera. We're not exactly innocent. We did hack into their systems."

"Tom, I'm going to make this as simple as I can. I don't care if we did steal it. We have the resources to bury them before it ever gets a trial."

Cutting Niera off, Tom says, "There's also the issue of the employees."

She stands and slams the table. "Were you born without a spine? The next time you get all gushy-eyed and waste my time over the termination of six thousand jobs, go home to your mama, or someone who gives a damn. Now get the hell out of here and make it happen!"

Once the room is empty, Drazen turns to Niera and says, "You seem tired. I hate to bring up one more thing for you to worry about."

"It's okay. Now that it's just you and me, I can manage anything, though I'm worried about the rebel groups... hackers...or whatever they call themselves."

Drazen informs her of a coordinated physical attack on several of their remote server locations earlier in the morning. "Fortunately, we intercepted them before suffering any material losses."

"That's good news," she says and then asks about Fitz. "I want him more involved. Tell him to be more creative finding the source of the attacks. Call him now!"

Drazen walks to the back of the room.

"Why are you going over there?" asks Niera.

"No need for you to be involved in these detail conversations." Drazen makes a call, speaking with a soft tone. "Look into everything, but protect our assets at all costs." After hanging up, Drazen calmly reassures Niera, "Fitz is handling it."

"Let's go to my office," she says. "There's something I want to show you." As they retreat through the back door, the cold space of the conference rooms turns dark.

# 7

# THE AUGMENTED INDIVIDUALISM PLATFORM

Niera opens a bottle of wine and takes a deep breath. "I feel so much calmer when I'm alone with you."

She hands Drazen a glass, then activates a three-dimensional computer display. "Now let's look at something more fulfilling."

After a series of voice commands, an icon appears on the screen: AIP. "The Augmented Individualism Platform. My life's work," she boasts before opening the program.

She gestures toward the display. "Look at this...we have almost nine billion active hosts and we're only days away from releasing our most powerful enhancements."

"That's remarkable," Drazen replies, eyebrow tilted, "but it's not only *your* life's work."

"Please don't go there. I know it's important to you. But to me, it's a tribute to what generations of my family have endured. My mission is to honor my family's service to world order."

*Endured? From within the grandest estates and surrounded by servants catering to every whim.* Drazen puts the glass of wine on the table. *I hate it when she forgets I don't drink!* "It certainly has been an exciting journey."

Niera sinks into the sofa, throwing her head back in exhaustion. "Why does the board seem to be turning on me? Our standing in the world has never been better, and the upcoming platform improvements will secure their family's safety and prosperity long past their lifetimes. I get the feeling some of them no longer trust me."

Drazen pauses. "You may be making more out of this than you need to. Every board member has multiple constituents to satisfy. When they're under pressure, it manifests itself in meetings as questions or critical comments. Your leadership has always been stellar, so don't take it personally."

"You're probably right. They simply don't remember how much we've overcome to be in the position we're in today. We have control throughout the world, and I'm getting ready to ensure all of our futures!"

"What do you mean? It sounds like there's something you're not telling me."

"It's nothing. I must be having what others would call a moment of weakness." Niera chuckles. "Do you remember how it all started?"

"Yes," he answers sharply.

"I'm sorry, of course you do. It makes the pressure seem lighter when we can talk about it."

Drazen sits beside Niera and takes her hand. "It feels

like a distant, warm memory. Go ahead, I always enjoy hearing you tell it," he says.

"It was twenty-five years ago. Rapid advancements in artificial intelligence, robotics, and physical sciences laid the groundwork for everything we built, but it all came together when the three of us solved the room-temperature quantum computing problem."

*You mean when John solved it,* Drazen thinks.

"Once we paired the exponential power of artificial general intelligence with quantum computing, our superintelligence models produced unprecedented gains in innovation and productivity across every industry. Food production improved. Medical care advanced. Sickness declined, and life expectancy rose worldwide. This new power reshaped society itself. Governments began acting as a unified body for the benefit of their citizens. It was a golden age for human civilization, and we were fortunate to sit at the table with GOD at the center of economic and political power."

Drazen cuts in. "At the same time, the population surged while artificial intelligence, robots, and humanoids replaced human labor. Productivity masked a deeper problem. It wasn't golden for everyone."

Niera exhales, then nods. "I'll concede that. Many struggled to adapt to the rapid pace of change. Without meaningful work, some fell into despair. Emotional hopelessness led to rising suicide rates. They couldn't see the bigger picture, and they failed to appreciate how the system benefited them. Even with their basic needs met, that growing lack of purpose became a threat. Global leaders recognized the risk to their own safety if the masses continued their downward spiral. Despair, loneliness, and lack of understanding breeds anger, and anger destabilizes order...not to mention the strain on world resources from a rapidly expanding nonproductive population."

*She's brilliant in her own right,* Drazen admits to himself. *And she does an excellent job managing all the internal and external conflicts.*

"And that's where you come in." he says.

"Well, where GOD comes in," she corrects. "We use the AIP to influence public opinion and behavior..."

"We've done a lot more than influence," Drazen interjects.

"To help people appreciate what they've been given," she replies evenly. "For their own good, of course."

Despite standing at the forefront of these advances, Drazen still marvels at the totality of change. The AIP permeates the lives of most of the world's population. People retreat into a digital world, living through their avatars while undergoing subtle...and sometimes...not-so-subtle cognitive conditioning. The system learns each host's desires and motivations, tailoring the messaging back with surgical precision. It's a brilliant mass-customization tool, powered by quantum processing and adaptive intelligence. The result is a population of passive servants with limited freedom in a system designed by an elite few.

"And you led the charge," Drazen says.

"I did lead the charge," Niera replies. "But I never imagined it would become this successful, and as addictive as it is. It began as a next-generation gaming platform, and it operated this way for years."

"Until quantum learning advanced far enough for

neurostimulators inside the ARC to replicate all five senses," Drazen says. "People could feel and experience anything within a digital environment without consequences or guilt. A gaming platform morphed into something else entirely. A social control system. People conceal their own imperfections while living idealized lives. And GOD provides it all for free."

Niera pauses. "That's quite an elaborate description," she says. "But there are limits to what a user's avatar can do. After all, we're still a civilized society. Users must play by the rules and, of course, opt into our marketing protocols. Do that, and they're free to experience what they want."

"The AIP and ARC are among the greatest intellectual achievements in history," Drazen says. "And as CEO, you leave nothing to chance, even creating your own avatar and regularly immersing yourself in the platform as any other host would."

Niera studies him. "How do you know how often I'm on the platform?"

Drazen twitches slightly. "I don't. I simply assume, as the leader, you do your own quality control, and there's no better way than firsthand experience."

She shakes her head. "Enough of the trip down memory lane. We can pat ourselves on the back all day long for building a product that nine billion hosts love, and global leadership needs, but none of it matters if we don't contain the hackers. We need Fitz to elevate his game."

# 8

## THE MUSCLE

A hacker sits alone at his desk. *It's just a matter of time.* He suffers a deep indent in his head from prolonged use of his headset. *The bigger you are, the less you pay attention to us little guys.* His head pans left to right across several displays looking for an opportunity, a weakness. His fingers initiate new attack code and launch it like waves of an amphibious military assault force. *This is interesting. The target is back. Let's find out who you are.*

The hacker's workstation gleams with an intricate array of hardware; all seamlessly integrated with AI software tools. His focus on the target waivers as intrusive thoughts creep in. "I need to connect to the AIP soon," he mutters. "I have to get back to my avatar, Ceasar. He's making his grand entrance tonight. I'll restart my hacking again tomorrow."

As the hacker puts on his ARC, his display freezes. A chilling image appears: his avatar, Ceasar hanging by his neck. Sweat ripples under the hacker's armpits, his lips clenched tight, and he's unable to enter any commands. Then the monitor fills with a blurred face; a hard man with a military haircut, graying goatee, square jaw, and a long scar running from the corner of his mouth to his eye.

"Who are you?" the hacker says.

The hard man speaks with a low and threatening voice. "I'm the man who has painted a target on your back…for all the fun you seemed to be having."

"Wha-wha-what do you mean?" the hacker says.

"The way I see it, you have two options," the hard man explains. "Option one, I'm the last person you talk to. Option two, I'm your best friend. It's your choice."

"What kind of choices are those?" the hacker asks.

The hard man growls and says, "Don't play games with me. I've been watching you for days, following your actions on and off the AIP. You have been trying to hack into our servers, and I have been letting you get close, learning what I need."

"You know nothing," the hacker yells back.

"I know you're a pawn at the end of the command chain, so why not become my pal and tell me who you work for, who's coordinating the attacks?" the hard man demands.

The hacker fidgets and takes a deep breath before responding. "I found the dirty little secret to the Farm, and I will share the 'harvest' with the rest of the world unless you release Ceasar and stay away from me forever."

"That's what I expected." The hard man smiles. "Now remember, in a harvest, one mustn't neglect the carrot for the corn."

The hacker looks confused and he mumbles, "You're just a guy on my screen. I'm not afraid of you. Tell me who you are."

Half a world away, the hard man pushes his chair away from the table. *Option one is my favorite, so much more satisfying...for me!* He's in a control room surrounded by rows of servers. His keyboard is hardwired directly into one of them. *I like to make a direct connection when dealing with these sensitive cases.*

He enters a command and watches as the hacker's ARC flashes, his back stiffens, and his eyes glaze over. The hard man says, "Another threat contained. Time to turn him into stew and pry what I need from his brain."

The hard man starts a game he has played countless times in the past, negotiating with himself as if there's someone else with even a slight bit of control over the outcome. He ponders a simple question. *Should I or shouldn't I turn it off? Why not flip a coin? Heads, I should and tails, I shouldn't.*

The coin comes down from its apex and settles into the cradled hands of the hard man. He lifts one finger and peeks at the result. *Heads, um...it's customary to start with a practice round. Let's try that again. Tails it is.*

The hard man leans back in his chair; eyes closed as the anticipation builds. Excited to pass along the results, he says, "Sorry, old boy, seems like your luck ran out with the coin flip. You see, if it had been heads, I would turn off your ARC's neuro pain stimulator, and you wouldn't feel any of this. Unfortunately for you, it was tails and you're going to feel everything. The good news for you is that I must be somewhere else in two hours."

A door with a restricted-location warning and GOD Corporation logo is partially ajar. From outside the control room looking in, Fitz is sitting in a portable chair, balancing his keyboard on his lap. Unlike his hard-man avatar, he's a small, demure person with closely cropped hair, watching coldly from a monitor, drink in hand. "Maybe two and a half hours," he says, looking at a half-full bottle of Jack. His body shakes as he begins working on the target.

An hour later, a knock on the door draws Fitz's attention. His lieutenant, Brass, a large man with a verifiably bad temper, stands inside the doorway. "Hey, boss, big boss wants to see you. Got a new ticket for you."

Fitz nods.

The lieutenant looks over at the monitor and sees the feed of the vegetative target. He winces, stating, "He's in bad shape, can't even scream. How cold."

"I have what I need. I can end this now," Fitz says. "Maximum power." Ten seconds later, the hacker is dead."

"This mind-fuck stuff is scary. I miss the old days of brute physical force," Brass says, slamming his fist on the desk.

Fitz replies, "In the world we live in today, force is a primitive weapon." He slaps the lieutenant's cheek. "But very much needed in some situations, which is when you come in handy."

# 9

## THE PATH PROGRAM

Farmer Johnson stands outside, enjoying the quiet moments before sunlight spills over the barn. With his eyes closed and chin raised, he inhales deeply, savoring the familiar blend of earthy soil, sweet blooming flowers, and the natural scents of animals mixed with hay. He finds himself yearning for the past. A time when his day would just be starting, with chores ahead and the smell of fresh-baked bread waiting at the conclusion of the workday.

He's on the driveway when he spots his neighbor on her porch. They make eye contact, but neither waves. Johnson rushes inside, logs onto the AIP, and notices an incoming message from "Suzanne Neighbor."

Her message says, "Couldn't talk outside. My avatar has something important to do, and I only have a few extra seconds."

"Me too. I just needed a quick stretch," he types in reply.

"The AIP's new features are great. They nailed the feeling." She responds.

"Yes, perfectly."

Johnson then blocks all other incoming messages from his neighbor. Moments later, he receives an invitation to be a beta tester for a prestigious new initiative called the Path Program. Honored to be recognized, he agrees immediately. Soon after, he sinks deeper into the AIP. He remains motionless except for muscles twitching and a visible bulge of excitement.

Meanwhile, in Suzanne's house, all four family members are home. Her husband, son, and daughter are sitting in different rooms, each of them wearing their ARC. Their respective avatars interact with family members regularly in the digital world.

In the physical world, the siblings pass each other in the kitchen looking for a quick snack but don't sit down or engage in any meaningful way other than a "hey" muttered by the sister.

Fighting the reflex to run back to his digital life, the brother musters a "what's up?" and heads down the hallway to his room.

His sister looks happy. *That's one more word than he spoke to me yesterday.* She scurries to her room as her avatar is about to start a girls' night out party.

# 10

## THE SPACESHIP

The X-series Delta spaceship completes a gravity assist orbit around Mars, stealing away a small amount of the red planet's kinetic energy to accelerate it to its destination, Jupiter's mysterious moon Europa. Its mission is to look for evidence of life.

The Daedalus symbol is printed on both sides of the sleek outer frame, accompanied by the stenciled letters "Icharus 9." The X-series incorporates new fusion ion thruster technology in addition to classified cryogenic and stem cell therapy chambers to allow for crewed planetary missions throughout the solar system.

Some conspiracy theorists claim the real intent of the X-series program is to explore space beyond our solar system, eventually reaching the planet that sent visitors crashing to Earth in the mid 1900s.

The spaceship is small by standards of past space-exploration vehicles, measuring one hundred fifty feet in length and weighing less than five million pounds. The exact specifications are top secret, but most informed people believe artificial intelligence along with quantum processing power improved the spacecraft's design, materials, and energy production.

Despite these improvements, the inside of the spacecraft is anything but luxury living. The real estate gained by shrinking the computer and engine compartments is more than made up for by an array of systems needed for extended space flight and SETI investigations. The interior shell is dotted with small windows, between which houses digital diagnostic terminals for essential operating systems and for measuring real-time interstellar threats from dangerous electromagnetic and gravitational waves.

Between the walls is a simple configuration of equipment, a single commander's chair, and dual, cryogenic life-support chambers. Although the X-series is designed for a single spacenaut, having two chambers is required as a safety measure.

At this point in the mission, the captain's chair remains empty. Its occupant, Commander Aria, lies in deep hibernation inside cryogenic chamber one. The small display in the corner of the chamber confirms all life-support readings to be normal.

Most of the journey will be managed by artificial intelligence due to the confined space within the X series, which could pose significant challenges related to loneliness and claustrophobia, even for the most qualified individuals. Commander Aria waits inside the chamber, her eyes closed until the designated wake-up time.

Green lights from the electromagnetic and

gravitational wave detectors reflect off the cryogenic chamber's clear cover, indicating no harmful radiation levels or gravitational waves detected. One of the ship's walls holds a large display with critical logistical information. The current readings show the distance from Earth, seventy-five million miles; the number of days remaining in cryogenic sleep, one hundred eighty-five; today's date, June 1, 2050; and the time, eighteen hundred thirty hours.

The gravity wave detector flashes orange for a moment, indicating an unexpected moderate-intensity gravity wave has passed through the ship. Other panels flicker and the ship rapidly decelerates, triggering the cryogenic chamber to begin its opening protocol. Within a second, all readings return to normal.

Ten minutes later, Commander Aria, a woman with piercing blue eyes, wakens, groggy and confused. *I'll never get used to waking from cryo. Now it's time to look at this beautiful moon.* She peers out the forward window at empty space. *That's strange, it should be right here.* She moves quickly to the rear window and sees the Sun. *Yes, you should be behind me, but you're much larger than you should be. What the hell is going on?*

She turns to the large display and sees that she has been awakened well before her arrival near Europa. She demands a status update from the artificial intelligence interface.

A female voice comes through the onboard communication system. "There were numerous temporary system disruptions, each of which I have already fixed. I can find no evidence of damage to the ship's structure.

Additionally, the life-support and propulsion systems are fully operational, and there are no harmful radiation levels. I await further instructions."

"Why was I awakened?" Aria fires off.

"I don't know yet. I'm running additional diagnostics."

Using the available windows and external camera feeds, Aria inspects the ship's exterior, confirming it's undamaged.

The artificial intelligence report beams across the ship's coms. "A significant gravity wave passed through the ship, impacting some of the quantum servers...although it theoretically should not have."

"Wait, that's not possible. There are no events in our surrounding space that could have accounted for the wave, even our Sun, as massive as it is."

"Agree, but with the caveat of known events."

Aria instructs the artificial intelligence to calculate where the wave came from and then tie into any available interstellar telescope system to confirm the analysis. "We need a smoking gun!"

The artificial intelligence triangulates the data and replies, "I have downloaded the information to the screen at the commander's chair."

Aria runs the data through a visualization program. *Colliding binary neutron stars. Two approaches fourteen days apart.* She is filled with a feeling of dread.

She jumps to her feet and radios Earth. "Austin, we have a problem. It's too late to warn you of the first wave, but there may be something much bigger coming your way in fourteen days."

Aria looks at the cabinet labeled "Quantum Servers." Inside are two rows of neatly packed server boxes, and on both sides of their black outer frame are the stenciled letters "GOD."

# 11

## THE FIRST WAVE

The streets of Los Angeles are typical of most large cities across the globe on an early-summer afternoon. Robotic cleaning equipment operates twenty-four hours a day, ensuring there is little trash on the ground and no graffiti on any façade.

Only a small percentage of the population is out, either ducking in and out of various retail locations not yet connected to the government's home-delivery infrastructure or taking a break from a captured life in their small apartments.

High-density city centers are the result of government incentives encouraging people to move back, touting safety, access to resources, and ease of communication. Conspiracy theorists say it's easier to create fear and keep people in their homes; a fact they support by the inverse relationship between personal interactions and population density.

On this day, June 1, 2050, people around the globe

are going about their routines, unaware that the most energetic gravitational wave in recorded history traveled through them. No one flinches or falls in pain. Humans are fortunate that each of their thirty trillion cells is too large to be affected by the event.

The same is not the case with the quantum computer systems running the world's retailers, banks, distribution networks, hospitals, and most everything else. These systems operate on a much smaller scale. They harness the power of the quantum revolution and rely on mysterious qubits for operation, and qubits are small enough to have "felt" the gravitational wave passing through Earth. Even though humans don't feel the wave directly, they're in the unfortunate position to bear the brunt of the issues from the quantum world disruption. Traveling at the speed of light, the wave passes through Earth in a heartbeat. Its devastation, however, lasts much longer.

The top cardiac surgery center is in the heart of the San Francisco city center. Staff and visitors move calmly through the halls knowing the greatest artificial learning models and precision robotics bring patient after patient home successfully.

In staging area one, a male patient lies on a table, his wife and daughter each holding one of his hands, the residue of dried tears visible on their faces.

"It's a routine valve replacement, no need to worry," the robotic hospital aide comments before moving him to the operating room.

Thirty minutes later, the supervising doctor leans over to the nurse and says, “The surgery is almost done, and much faster than when we operated with these,” holding up his hands.

Suddenly, the IV pump and ventilator alarms start flashing and the operating room loses its data feed. “Cut the power,” screams the doctor as the robotic surgical arm slices through the patient’s heart. They look at each other confused, horrified.

The nurse whimpers and says, “Doctor, what can we do? Should I perform CPR?”

“It’s too late,” the doctor says, looking down. “Please ask the family to meet me in the grieving room.” Minutes later, the doctor wipes his eyes before reaching for the handle.

In South Africa, a diplomat and his family sit comfortably in the front car of the high-speed Maglev train. Their first-class tickets cap off a day spent at the last remaining wildlife park available to the general public.

“Dad, how fast can this train go?” the young girl asks.

“If they push it, more than four hundred and fifty miles per hour.”

“So cool,” she says.

Her brother approaches the glass window trying for a better view of the ground flying below him. He sees something concerning and asks his mom, “Do you see the light in front of us? It seems to be on our train’s guideway, and it’s coming at us fast.”

The mom looks up to see fear in the eyes of the

passengers in the first car of the train coming at them. Her mouth opens, but there's no time to scream before the trains collide.

In Chicago, warm glowing lights illuminate the living room as a woman tries to engage her avatar on the AIP. Nearby, drinks and snacks are conveniently arranged to help her stay comfortable during a long session. After putting on her ARC, she receives an error message. A cold sweat forms on her brow as she tries repeatedly to get access. Her hands tremble and her eyes well up with tears when the platform confirms her avatar no longer exists. *I've lost everything. I'm planning to get married tonight, and he's so handsome.* All emotion leaves her face. She walks to her bedroom, unlocks a small metal case, and grabs the contents. A few seconds later, the room explodes with the sound of a single gunshot.

# 12

## THE PREDICTION

Alyssa lies on the couch, observing the lights of the sprawling urban center from the high-rise suite that her father's financial advisor convinced her to buy. Her living room smells like dessert, a familiar combination from the afternoon peppermint tea and strawberry syrup poured generously over vanilla ice cream earlier in the evening.

Though not often anymore, she thinks about how much she has changed. When her parents were alive, she tried not to take advantage of their wealth, often rejecting personal luxuries so as not to alienate even more of the locals. When she met him, she grew fonder of the finer things in life...for the material things. In what used to cause a tsunami of shame, she now feels only slight guilt for the fact that her furniture and décor cost more than the average family's annual income and that her residence could easily house many of the city's homeless population. Her eyes close so she can focus. Her thoughts wind up in the same place as always. *I should reconsider who I have become, but not tonight.*

Across the room, her tabby cat, Maya, roams free, exploring the dozen rooms Alyssa rarely walks into. On warm evenings, like tonight, Maya spends time alone on the outdoor patio while her owner doesn't look up from the work she's brought home. *I hate being grounded here, but the university felt it was in the best interest of the students and faculty to cancel classes after yesterday's mysterious events.*

Alyssa looks for a place to set her computer on the coffee table but finds the space cluttered with dirty kitchen dishware, last season's holiday decorations, and several business files. *I need a bigger table, or just leave it on the floor... nothing covering that except a dozen displaced throw pillows.* She laughs at the obvious disarray of her condominium.

Stepping around various obstacles, she navigates the full length of the building's top floor to open a large window in her kitchen. The wind whips through the opening and topples a stack of pictures on the table, kicking up some dust and cracking the frame on one of them. *The ex would not like that, although he certainly deserves it, and more.* Alyssa places a pile of unopened mail over the pictures and turns to Maya. "Too bad you're not a maid. You could earn your keep around here."

*As long as I'm in the kitchen, I may as well make something to eat.* She reads the labels her personal chef affixed to each meal. *Tough decision. I may need some liquid help before I pick one.* She pulls a bottle out of the custom wine chiller and places it in the automated wine opener. A few seconds later, a flashing red light indicates the cork has broken. *You would think, for $1,500 a bottle, this would not happen.*

After a quick bite and a healthy second pour of wine, Alyssa is back on the couch ready to work. *Where to begin? Do I start with the old and climb up, or the new and climb down?* A ping announces a new email titled "Urgent, New Satellite Array Binary Neutron Star Data." *This must be from our hydrogen gas cloud observations. New emails it is.*

She opens the report and reads it twice, unconsciously sitting up after the first pass. Although she has not always been confident or correct in life's personal situations, very few times has she ever been wrong, or even surprised, in professional ones. Alyssa huffs in disbelief. She knows her team looked at it many years ago, albeit with an inferior satellite and in different wavelengths, and it was normal. Nothing more than a giant cloud of hydrogen gas and trace amounts of other elements. She connects with her artificial intelligence assistant, Luis.

"Hey, Luis, your humor modules are disabled, so how can you be punking me with this report?"

"Ms. Starr, I'm not playing a game. I found it in the data a few minutes ago."

"What do you mean you found it?"

Luis replies, "I was making our initial observations of the gas cloud in the usual frequencies of the electromagnetic spectrum and didn't see anything different from past observations. But when I switched one of our satellites over to the new gravitational wave detectors, I saw the anomaly."

"Please explain what anomaly you saw."

"Readings were normal, and then I detected a significant gravitational wave. It was gone in an instant, but I accessed data from our other two satellites and triangulated the source. I found the neutron stars."

"Luis, hundreds of observations have been made of this gas cloud, and no one has called out anything like a neutron star."

"Yes, but it's a dense cloud, and past observations have focused on the electromagnetic spectrum. Also, we know our satellite array is different. It's positioned a billion miles beyond the sun, equipped with eighth-generation artificial intelligence software, state-of-the-art gravitational wave detectors, and most importantly, an array of three individual satellites. All three satellites are a million miles apart, providing optimal observational data on the hydrogen cloud.

Alyssa's voice quivers with uncertainty. "I want to be sure I have this right. Our gravitational wave detectors recorded an unusually large wave, which we triangulated back to the source and found the unique magnetic footprint for a neutron star in a suspected inert gas cloud?"

Luis responds, "Not just one neutron star but an unstable binary pair!"

"How do you know they're unstable?" Alyssa asks.

"Because of the gravitational wave's magnitude. If they were in a stable orbit, the waves would be too small to be an issue. Something happened to create the massive wave."

Alyssa leans back, holding her hands over her face. "Luis, we have a problem. I need to speak with someone else. Thank you, and goodbye."

"Call Mr. Singh," Alyssa shouts to the virtual assistant.

Mr. Singh answers in his usual soft, calm tone. "Hello, Ms. Starr, to what do I owe the pleasure of this call?"

"Mr. Singh, I don't want to be rude, but I have an urgent question for you, given your expertise in neutron star life cycles."

"Okay, yes, go on."

"I'm forwarding to you an analysis of a binary neutron star system. Open it and let me know your thoughts." Alyssa's voice shakes as she makes the request.

"I have it. Give me a couple minutes."

*What's taking so long? Get a grip, it's only been thirty seconds. It feels like an hour.* She paces across the room, shaking her arms to dissipate her nervous energy.

"Ms. Starr, I've looked at the data. Where are these two neutron stars located, and when did your satellite array register the gravitational wave?"

"They're ten light-years away, and they registered the wave yesterday. We only looked at the data a short while ago."

"That seems impossible. We should have known about something that close."

"No one has looked at this hydrogen gas cloud for years. It's considered empty by the scientific community and a dead end for any ongoing research. I only did it to allow for real-time refining of some artificial intelligence software I was testing."

Mr. Singh says, "The gravitational wave you detected is the result of an initial, mild impact. Think of it like two people running toward each other on a street and, when they're close enough, their arms collide, causing their bodies to change velocity and position. With this pair of neutron stars, the initial impact changed their orbital dynamics, locking them on an inexorable path to total collapse. In their final minutes, the two stars' orbital velocity will increase to a small percentage of the speed of light. And then their ultimate collision will cause a massive explosion, sending out a second gravitational wave more powerful than Earth has experienced since the dawn of human civilization."

"When?"

"As you know, we're seeing things as they were at some point in the past. This collision has already happened out in space. These neutron stars are ten light-years away, so it has taken this first gravitational wave ten years to reach your detector. The actual event is over."

"I understand, but how much time is there between the initial impact and the final collision?"

"I suspect you already know the answer, Ms. Starr. Am I correct?"

"Yes. I ran it through our astrophysics' quantum program, and it came back with fourteen days, two hours, and thirty minutes, give or take a few minutes."

"So, Ms. Starr, you should expect your satellite array to receive the second gravitational wave...the one from the final collision in that time period. And based on where your satellites are located, Earth will experience the wave approximately ninety-eight minutes after your satellites."

After several seconds of silence, Mr. Singh says to Alyssa, "I'm sure the silence is because you're calculating the order of magnitude increase in gravitational wave energy the final collision will create compared to the initial impact."

"Exactly, and it's almost done."

"Ms. Starr, I must go. My building's fire-prevention systems mysteriously failed yesterday, just like so many other systems throughout the world, and I need to bring it back online. Don't bother finishing your calculation. I can tell you from similar binary neutron star collisions it will be a thousand times the magnitude."

"Confirmed!"

# 13

## THE RESPONSE

The fervor is building among the throngs of reporters representing every news outlet gathered outside the headquarters of GOD. Each one of them is vocally clambering over the other as they try to get their questions answered from the GOD official standing outside the locked doors. A mousy man sent from on high is taking a public beating, but that is what punching bags are used for, after all.

"As I have stated numerous times, our team has identified a glitch and is in the process of fixing it," exclaims the representative, which does nothing to assuage the crowd but send them further into a noisy rabble that is audible to the GOD employees up to the fifteenth floor. But that is fine, as the penthouse office of Niera Kristain is a good forty floors above the crowd; the only protests she hears are those of the wind and crows.

Inside her penthouse office, she sits in a leather and carbon-fiber throne specifically designed for each contour of her body. Niera gives a command, and the full wall of windows darkens before transforming into a twenty-foot monitor where she views the last part of the mousy man's press conference. She chuckles with delight seeing him take the abuse. She then switches channels to see Senator Cortez standing in the rotunda of the capital in front of a bevy of microphones and eager journalists.

Senator Cortez raises her hands as if calming a group of rowdy middle-schoolers on a field trip. "People, people, people, I assure you, as head of the Global Economics and Development Committee, we've already dispatched a task force to look into these issues and found nothing alarming or out of the ordinary." The senator pauses to take a breath as the crowd erupts, as she knew they would. Raising her voice, she says, "And I can tell you, initial reports of coordinated hackers is nothing short of fake news. Anomalies and accidents happen, and they happen all over the world. To assume there's any suspicious connection is a fallacy. This is simply a coincidence and a matter of fiction...science fiction, most likely."

"Good girl," Niera states to the room, empty but for her. She changes the frequency one more time to see herself on the screen, sitting virtually at a polished wooden table before a panel of United Nations members. Her name tag, "Niera Kristain, Head of Global Operation Design," flickers in front of her. The bottom of the ticker reads yesterday's date.

She starts her viewing just after the chairperson has tried, in vain, to publicly lash her for a myriad of international matters, lack of visibility and transparency from GOD, insufficient communication, and a litany of other concerns.

"Do you realize how much the world has invested in your company and the duty we have to protect our citizens?" the chairperson asks.

"Madam Chairperson, I'm well aware of the position and power my company has throughout the world. May I remind you this body's new international trading platform is close to going online, and I would hate to spend more time in administrative meetings when I should be back at GOD signing off on its release." And with that, Niera pushes herself away from the table and walks out of the meeting to the stunned and apoplectic silence of the room.

She has just enough time to applaud her previous day's performance before the feed is interrupted. A blinking red graphic reads, "Incoming call: GOD BOARD EMERGENCY MEETING."

Niera huffs, takes a breath, and verbalizes, "Accept."

None of the board members begin with introductions or niceties, launching directly into a demand to know what went wrong two days ago. Niera waits for the initial salvo to stop and calmy replies, "It was a momentary blip."

Joining the meeting from the top deck of his luxury yacht, an agitated board member says, "A blip, Ms. Kristain? Five thousand are dead globally, with more likely if we do not resolve the discrepancies soon. Supply chains are disrupted, our AIP is at risk, and rogue groups are harassing our servers. And that's a blip to you?"

"Five thousand out of twelve billion. Not to sound too callous, but that kind of percentage is still ten times smaller than the margin of error for validating any of our systems. In respect to the rogue groups, our server farms encircle the world. An elephant doesn't alter the course of her herd based on the threat of an ant, does she?"

With the board silenced, she continues. "Our work is revolutionizing the world, the way our species lives, works, and thrives. Thanks to us, life expectancy has risen by twenty percent. You chastise me about five thousand deaths but say nothing of the life and pleasure we've given to these twelve billion people. I implore all of you to think about that the next time you greet your parents, grandparents, or great-grandparents."

"No one greets anyone anymore. They're all brain-dead, sitting on the all-too-valuable life-sucking platform," one of the board members utters under her breath.

Niera leans forward to stare at the board members hovering in front of her in a panoramic swath. *I hear every word, and I can also see the slight movement of your lips, Mrs. Grantham.*

Niera continues her rationale. "Do I need to remind you this life-sucking platform pays the mortgages on your third and fourth homes, and assures stability of the communities you live above, Mrs. Grantham?"

Adjusting her camera to ensure everyone can see her clearly, Niera states, "As for the rest of you, this journey has involved stages where small sacrifices were necessary for the greater good. You can tell yourself and your family whatever you need to sleep at night, but don't bullshit me and pretend you weren't aware. I don't remember anyone having a moral meltdown as we achieved the progress we promised."

The man on the yacht makes a comment in a defeated

tone. "It's still a lot of people, Niera, and we never know when it may directly impact someone who can cause us trouble."

Niera fires back, "A lot of people? At the current birth rates, it takes seventeen minutes and thirty-two seconds to replace five thousand lives. Since the start of this meeting twenty-two minutes ago, we're very much back in the black." Not bothering to wait to hear the board's response or listen to any additional questions, she says, "Goodbye," and ends the call with a disrespectful push of a button.

Rising from her throne, she stretches, feeling her knee joint crack and pop. *That's not supposed to happen. My last injection of CartiBots was only a few months ago. Longevity for nanoparticle treatments is something else I need to get the R&D team to improve upon.*

Niera moves from her desk to the kitchen of her on-site residence. She withdraws a foil-wrapped package from the refrigerator, with the words "GOD Bar" printed in a familiar font. Niera removes the top, revealing the unappetizing gray rectangle, and devours it in two bites. She snaps her fingers, suddenly remembering an important piece of business, and presses her temple to contact Fitz.

He picks up quickly, as he knows he must always do. "What can I do for you, big boss?"

"You can start by stopping calling me ridiculous names."

"Got it, Ms. Kristain."

"Fitz, have you been drinking?"

"Would you deny me a little ale, given all the secrets I help you protect?" he says in a tone Niera does not appreciate.

"Fitz, listen carefully. Mrs. Grantham mumbled an ill-advised comment toward the end of our call. Can you please stop by and discuss it with her?"

Fitz looks at his distorted reflection in the whiskey bottle. "Do you want me to make it quick?" His body is shaking, hoping he gets the answer he wants.

"I want you to reeducate her," Niera replies. "Your methods are your own."

Fitz's gravelly voice doesn't hesitate. "Done."

Niera's personality switches as she calls in her assistant, pulling back on the confident, everything-is-under-control attitude she's been projecting to the UN, the board, the press, and anyone else outside the spheres of GOD.

Her assistant, Jacob, a young man hoping enough "yes, ma'ams" will scurry him up the corporate ladder, emerges from the door to the lobby. "Do you need anything before the next call, Ms. Kristain?"

"Yes, Stephen. I need you to find out what the holy hell is happening with the investigation."

Before correcting her, Jacob takes a deep breath to lower his blood pressure. He thinks of the future when she will be compelled to appreciate his skills. He then exhales using the force of his breath to shout, "It's Jacob, ma'am."

"It's 'breadline' if you don't find me some goddamned answers."

Jacob hesitates before speaking, aware that his next statement may not be well received. "We still do not have the information, ma'am. We're waiting on diagnostics to come back."

"Does anyone get their job done around here? Where is our illustrious engineer? Find him and tell him he better have some answers, and soon."

"I'll head there myself."

"No, send Fitz. I want him to know I'm serious."

His feelings hurt, Jacob slinks away. As he approaches the back door, a sharp cry from Niera causes him to turn back. "Everything okay, ma'am?" Jacob asks, seeing she's clutching her eye.

He instinctively moves toward her, but she stops him with an outward hand, turning from him like a vampire would a mirror. "I don't need your help removing an eyelash from my eye," she screams.

"Of course, ma'am. If there's nothing else..."

"Nothing."

"I'll inform Fitz of his directives." He gulps as the word "Fitz" leaves his mouth, like a mouse forced to utter the word "snake."

With Jacob gone and the room empty but for herself, Niera enters the bathroom. Standing at the sink, she opens her palm, gazing at the brown contact lens withered inside. She looks in the mirror, at the heterogeny of her gaze: one eye a deep umber, the other a shimmering blue.

Niera applies a few drops of saline, rehydrating the lens, and pops it back in place, the face in the mirror once more projecting the guise with which she confronts the world.

# 14

## THE INVESTIGATION

Most employees coming through the front door of the GOD building verify their biometric data, walk through a weapons sensor, get on the elevator, and push one of the forty buttons on the "going up" side of the elevator panel. The remaining employees are the lucky ones, heading to the below-ground offices of the quantum engineering team. Lucky at least from the perspective of their leader, Matt Boson.

On this day, a dozen members arrive at 6:45 a.m., the office lights emanating a bright-yellow hue indicative of their being on for at least sixty minutes. The smell of strong brewed coffee delights their senses as they each pour a cup and settle into their respective workstations.

Each station is outfitted with either an advanced pressure-technology chair or ergonomic posture balls. Both choices help to reduce fatigue and stimulate blood flow for cognitive enhancement.

"Good morning, help yourself to some coffee," a voice from the back bellows out.

An engineer leans over and whispers to their work mate, "He didn't look up long enough to see we'd already helped ourselves."

"Did you really expect something different?"

"No, but we love the guy anyway."

"Agreed."

Matt sits in the back office pouring over lines of code, scrutinizing them, trying to figure out what affected their servers. Already at it for a couple of hours, his eyes look more like a paramedic's after a full work shift. His body language reveals both an excitement to solve an unknown problem and concern he may not, alternating in rhythm like the oscillating fields of an electromagnetic wave.

The clock chimes 8:00 a.m. when Fitz quietly enters from a side staircase rather than the elevator. This is a common strategy for him, as it provides a better chance of being unnoticed and seeing something useful.

The loud greeting from the closest team member hangs in the air, signaling both his arrival and the undercurrent of anxiety that accompanies it.

Fitz's footsteps echo against the tiled floor, the rhythm briefly disrupting the steady hum of the morning workflow. As he moves through the room, team members become tentative and their finger movements decrease in speed and purpose as if inserted into molasses.

One engineer straightens in her chair and fixes her eyes on her artificial intelligence's analysis with exaggerated focus.

Fitz's gaze sweeps deliberately from one desk to the next,

lingering just long enough to make each person aware of his scrutiny. A few team members exchange nervous glances, while others pretend to be utterly absorbed in their work.

"Hey, boss, we have a visitor," Eugene says.

Matt replies, "Last thing we need right now."

Fitz snarls and greets Matt. "Good to see you too, Boson. Now tell me something about the situation that will make me happy."

"As far as I can tell, it's not our coding. It's some sort of widespread external influence."

Fitz fires back, "No shit. They're called hackers."

"Don't be stupid, Fitz. What we're seeing here is both too uniform and too random. It was widespread and prolific, spanning multiple languages, and then it disappeared as swiftly as it had emerged. One organized hacker group could not implement all of this on its own, and yet every instance across the globe is identical and timed at the exact same microsecond."

"I don't care about your hypothesis. My bet is still on the same set of rebels trying to disrupt our server farms around the globe. To me, they're all hackers!"

"Be more logical, Fitz. Hackers need some kind of payoff, which is why they focus on financial, technological, or political institutions. The recent disruptions disproportionately impacted small-time, individual interests on lower levels of our advanced quantum systems. And why did they stop without making any demands? Our systems were in trouble. Several orders of magnitude more and they could have attacked our higher-level infrastructure. You know, the stuff your boss and his associates care the most about. What we're looking at isn't a human attack."

"And you're the expert at spotting human motivation, are you?" Fitz says sarcastically. "No, you're missing something. Do we need someone with a little more intellect to step in? Should I ask Drazen to help?" he asks, directly challenging Matt's abilities.

Eugene steps in front of Fitz. "Relax, Matt will figure it out, and you should try being happy for a change. Who knows, it might stick."

Fitz angles his scarred cheek toward Eugene and snarls more like an animal than a human. "If I don't look happy to you now, just wait."

Matt fires back at Fitz, "Quit threatening my team and get the hell out of our lab. Your presence is not helping anyone."

Fitz chuckles. "Seems I've gotten under your skin." On his way out, he comments, "A guy like me does not make threats without looking forward to acting on them. Now, do your jobs and I will leave you alone. If not, I'll be your worst nightmare."

The engineers wait for Fitz to be far enough away before poking fun at him. Eugene comments, "That cranky bastard. I'm sure he would be a lot happier if he got his scar fixed. Doesn't he know we could fix it for him in a fifteen-minute outpatient procedure?"

An engineer in the back says, "The irony that our head of security is a closet Luddite is too much for me to bear." He looks at Matt, trying to get him to join in the conversation. But Matt is lost in his work again, or just not interested.

All the team can see is a furrowed brow and random hand gestures as he dives even deeper into the coding.

# 15

## THE EX-HUSBAND

Alyssa stands in the middle of a circular lecture room showing her students images and computer simulations of black holes and the Spaghettification theory when, midway through her presentation, a call interrupts her lecture.

The caller details on her watch show "June 4 incoming from Daedalus." *Perfect timing, as always!* She rejects the call, apologizing to her class, and continues with the lecture.

Moments later, another call comes in. Embarrassed, she slams the watch into a drawer, which spontaneously causes a connection to the classroom sound system. A private message broadcasts to the class a moment later.

A student jokes, "Looks like the teacher is getting a booty call from her ex."

Before she can respond, Gaio Estrella's face appears on the screen. "I'm sorry to break in like this, but we need to talk," the CEO of the Daedalus Space Exploration Company says beseechingly.

*If I had a dollar for every time he prioritized his life over mine, I'd be...well, even more rich.* Alyssa pushes back. "I'm in the middle of my class. Don't you remember our previous discussion on maintaining proper boundaries?"

Gaio says, "I do. It pains me to disrupt your class considering the great work you're doing, and I offer an apology to everyone there. My issue is one of national security, and I'm not here to talk to my ex-wife. I'm here to talk to a world-renowned astrophysicist. If you know someone with those credentials, her expertise is desperately needed."

There's a collective "Ouch" as Gaio's face goes dark.

After class, Alyssa calls Gaio. "How did you get access to my lecture hall's communications, and who the hell do you think you are, putting me in that position in front of my students?"

"I'm sorry, Alyssa. It's Saturday and I did not expect you would be in class."

"Our honors class has an extra session one Saturday per month. I suppose we're lucky you chose the same day to barge in."

"I didn't know who else to call, and this is a matter of extreme urgency. Three days ago, one of my interplanetary spacecrafts was damaged. After reviewing the details this weekend, I believe a fire is still burning."

*Well then put it out, Einstein.* "Gaio, I'm here on Earth, so what do you want me to do, and what specifically are you talking about?"

"You were always great at finding solutions, even

when the facts were messy. I would like you to hear this directly from the source." Gaio replays last Wednesday's communications log with the spacenaut.

Alyssa listens, but before it finishes, she tells Gaio, "You can turn it off."

"But it's not done. There's more of the picture to fill in."

"To borrow one of your favorite analogies, all the strokes of the brush are finished. I know what is coming!"

# 16

## THE SCENT

Back at the quantum solutions lab, a female engineer keeps one eye on her 3D terminal and the other on the clock. As it changes to 7:00 p.m. she glances up, getting a silent nod from several of her associates before asking the question. “Hey, Matt, it’s Saturday night and a few of us are going out. Would you like to have a drink with us?”

“I’m sorry, I can’t tonight,” he replies quickly.

Another team member comments to the female engineer, “Why do you even ask anymore?”

“Because we’re quantum coders, everything is possible, and someday the answer’s bound to be beyond the wall of no.” The pair laugh at the inside joke.

Jacob, Niera’s assistant, enters the lab quietly and asks, “What are you laughing at?”

“Oh, hi, Jacob. Just a joke you wouldn’t understand.”

A look of disdain flashes across his eyes but shifts to excitement as he delivers unwelcome news. “What I’m about to tell you is not a joke. Niera has grounded your team until you have an answer to our recent troubles."

Matt objects, "They all have lives, and we're working all weekend as it is."

"Maybe so, but Niera doesn't care. She will terminate their jobs if you don't agree." Jacob doesn't wait for pushback. "So it's your choice."

Eugene looks at Matt. "I know you want to defend us, but it's not your fault. We'll be comfortable in corporate housing until this all blows over."

Another team member chimes in. "It's not like any of us are married. We spend most of our time together anyway."

Matt says, "Thanks, everyone. Why don't you all go home and come back with the things you need? I'll be right behind you, and then I'll see you back here in the morning." *I need to say this loud enough for everyone to hear, especially Jacob.* "Yes, I do believe she's a bitch."

As the last team member walks out, Matt switches his thoughts back to the issues at hand. *This is going to be a late night.* He clicks the reorder button under the kitchen icon and, five minutes later, a delivery bot arrives with his favorite hot meal. *Now that's efficient. If they only had a bathroom bot, I'd never have to move from my chair.*

Five hours later, Matt is surprised to hear the midnight bell and change of days. *Have I really been here that long? I must have brewed the first pot over eighteen hours ago.* His current cup is as cold as the lab. The custom lighting is designed to mimic sunlight, but it doesn't fool anyone. After so many hours, the yellow haze is suffocating.

For the last two hours, Matt has moved from analyzing the code to digging deep into the system architecture looking for something, anything, to give him a clue. *What am I expecting to find? I designed this whole environment.* Matt's body language changes, straightening in his chair and then standing to stimulate blood flow and get rid of the tingling in his legs.

Two figures watch Matt from an emergency-exit doorway above the lab. One of the onlookers steps forward through the exit door, interested in Matt's sudden level of excitement.

"This is strange," Matt mumbles under his breath. "Never seen this before, and they're drawing enormous amounts of energy." His heart pounds. *They're buried in two classified nonproduction servers, but each has consistent output, so they're very much live.* Speaking toward the three-dimensional diagrams, he says, "Why would someone designate you as nonproduction, and what are you hiding inside?"

Wiping sweat from his hands, Matt makes a few attempts to access the servers. *Whoever built this must have something valuable to hide. I'm being repeatedly denied, even with my clearance. Time to up the game and try some of the hacking tools our company "allegedly" uses on the competition.*

Matt engages a quantum hacking key and finds a back door into the server's directory. *The Path Program and the Farm. They're programs using a vast amount of processing power, even more than our most advanced quantum computers. How can this be?* "Now what is this...an 'opt-in' protocol?" he says. But before he can go further, he's interrupted.

Matt adjusts his output from 3D to his computer screen and then puts it in a temporary sleep mode out of view as Fitz and Drazen enter the lab. *I'm not sure whether the scent of Jack Daniel's or expensive cologne hit me first, but I'm glad they're both pungent.*

Drazen sits without saying a word as Fitz stumbles around opening drawers and reading the team's activity files, trying to force Matt into a confrontation.

Matt rolls his eyes, leans forward, and says, "You're wasting my time. And, Fitz, you look like you're ready to fall. How many swigs has it been tonight?"

Drazen confronts Matt. "Have you found the bug or the hacker?"

"No, nothing since your lapdog graced our presence this morning."

Fitz replies, "Sometimes you just need a little outside help...or influence."

Smiling, Matt responds, "You are the one needing outside help, and a lot of it!"

Fitz rambles about loyalty and boasts about always getting his man. "It goes better for guilty parties when they come clean early. There's less need to apply higher levels of persuasion."

Matt ignores him, not allowing himself to be baited.

Drazen asks Matt, "Does the encryption security in our quantum computers make it impossible for anyone or anything from the outside to hack our systems?"

Matt sighs. "In theory, yes. But the same tools..."

Fitz interrupts. "What were you looking at before we came in?" He watches for some type of guilty tell in Matt's reaction; dilating pupils, drops of sweat, or shivering knees.

Matt remains calm and gives him a bullshit technical answer. He then pushes the chair back with force, closes his working session, and locks his access. Before exiting the lab, Matt says, "I have to go. Please let yourselves out."

Midway down the hall, Matt's thoughts shift away from his unwelcome guests to visiting a more friendly face from the past.

Drazen approaches Fitz, asking, "Why do you seem so entertained by all of this? His response is perplexing to me."

"I like swatting at them, waiting for them to make a mistake. Like a cat does to a bug on the floor."

Drazen opens Matt's workstation. "What do you think he uses as his password?"

"Let me save you some time. Boson is as tight as they come. You shouldn't expect to break his access."

"They all consider themselves the smartest. It's a flaw to exploit." Drazen's fingers move across the control device like he's performing Mozart on a piano. "Success. This is the last thing Boson saw." He turns the screen toward Fitz.

"Wow, you're more resourceful than I gave you credit for. You will have to teach me that someday."

"You have a hard head, Fitz, which is why you're tops at what you do. Leave the creative thinking to me and stay in your lane."

Fitz's fists tighten before he asks, "Did he get in?"

"No, neither of them has been breached...yet." He gives Fitz a cold stare. "You realize the extent of our problems, don't you?"

Fitz answers, "Of course. We have an inside rat. I'll engage the typical assets for extermination."

# 17

## THE MENTOR

Matt's eyes are closed; his head turned sixty degrees toward the small window on his left. His lips are moving, betraying the conversation he's having with himself. He doesn't hear the ding followed by the captain's announcement: "There are reports of turbulence ahead, so we've turned on the seat belt sign. Please return to your seats immediately and buckle in."

Matt's eyes open enough to locate the crackers and orange juice in his seat pocket; both are needed to quell his churning stomach. *Technically, it's the weekend, so her lockdown orders shouldn't go into effect until Monday, right?* Unable to convince himself, he expects to be on the long end of Niera's wrath when he gets back.

He feels something poking him in the side and turns his head toward seat 15B. The passenger in the middle seat is staring at him, arms crossed, and in a curt tone, says, "Seems you're deep in thought. Not sure if you could hear the announcement to buckle your seat belt," pointing into Matt's lap.

"Thank you, I was distracted." Matt turns his head back toward the window.

"Is this a work or fun trip?" 15B blurts out.

Matt rolls his eyes before turning back. *Please leave me alone. Isn't it obvious I have no interest in chatting with you, unless you like the smell of puke in your lap?* "It's work." He hopes his quick answer will be enough.

"Me too. What are you flying for?" 15B says as he finishes his fourth bag of free cookies.

*I thought sitting next to you and making nice-nice conversation would be great fun on a Sunday, so I booked a ticket and picked this seat!* "I'm visiting my college mentor hoping she will help me solve some challenges I'm having at work."

The captain's voice comes through again. "We're starting our descent and will be on the ground shortly."

*Saved by the bell.*

The car-rental line is longer than expected, giving Matt time to reflect on his past relationship with Jenna Zane. *Why have we only spoken a few times over the past ten years? We became close, even more so than I would have expected, given she wasn't my formal collegiate advisor, just Alyssa's. I wonder how Alyssa is doing. It was both our faults. Life became so complicated. I never told her how much...and then she married that guy!*

• • •

Matt sits perched in the driver's seat of the convertible, confident in his decision to upgrade from a basic economy and avoid the self-driving options. *I have traveled to Berkeley's campus a hundred times, and I'm always impressed by the beauty of this area.* He turns up the radio's volume, but it's no use, as the sound is drowned out by the wind blowing across his face.

As he arrives at the faculty advisor building, his hands tingle at the memory of late-night conversations and the genuine friendship the three of them once shared. *She always worked in her office on Sundays. I hope she hasn't changed her routine.*

Matt makes his way through a series of marble-lined hallways to the same door he frequented while finishing his advanced studies. Like a sprinter getting into the blocks, he shakes his arms to get rid of any last nerves. *Is it a bad idea to show up without giving her a heads-up? No, whenever I needed her in the past, she was there...notice or not. Yet this feels different. We're adults, peers...so much has happened.*

Matt's knuckles contact the door just below the nameplate "Jenna Zane, Student Mentor." A familiar voice responds, "Yes, come in. It's not locked."

His sweaty palms make it difficult to turn the handle, and when he peeks through the opening, he sees a woman reading an old book at her desk. "I hope you're still giving out advice to struggling souls," Matt says.

Jenna straightens in her chair, eyes wide open, and spins around to see Matt. A smile covers her face as she closes the distance between them, giving Matt a long hug. "I'm so happy to see you, even without an appointment."

As the embrace loosens, Matt notices the familiar, sweet smell of lavender emanating from the variety of candles placed around the room. The walls are colored in natural earth tones, and the artwork seems to be the same as when he left the school, only organized in a different pattern.

Jenna doesn't look a day older than on graduation day: black hair without even a touch of gray, no wrinkles, same youthful skin, and an energetic demeanor. He says, "You look amazing. The years have taken their toll on me, but you look exactly the same."

Jenna fumbles before responding. "It must be something in the water." She laughs softly, her eyes crinkling with familiar warmth as she settles back into her chair. After a few minutes of shared pleasantries, Jenna leans forward with elbows on her desk and says, "Now, I'm sure you didn't come here just to compliment an older lady."

"You're right. I'm here because I have an unsolvable work problem, yet I know there are no unsolvable problems, just inadequate solutions." Matt slumps into a chair. "Sometimes I wish our systems didn't run the world."

"Why don't you take a breath and start at the beginning." Jenna turns the out of office sign on and says, "I don't expect too many visitors on a Sunday, but I have a feeling this will require our undivided attention. Now, what specifically is the problem?"

Matt describes the issues, and Jenna chimes in. "We had several problems with the systems on the campus also. The administrators informed us that it was a one-time issue, and your company representatives confirmed that it was resolved. There have been no other problems since then, so we took it as the truth."

"The truth! The truth is, we have no idea what happened. It's not an issue with the code, the servers are stable, there have been no successful external hacks, and we cannot replicate the issues. It's like a ghost came in, screwed around with our quantum environment, and then disappeared without a trace."

"You work for GOD. The company has unlimited talent and resources. Certainly there are other people who can help. What about your superiors?"

Matt bites his lip. "They think we're being outsmarted by external resources or it's some type of internal sabotage. Their patience is thin, and I don't have any meaningful leads to pursue. They even sent their chief enforcer down to rattle my team. For now, he's only making demands, but I know him and it can escalate quickly if I don't find something. Either way, I'm in their crosshairs and, for the first time in my life, I can't find an earthly solution to a problem." Matt leans back in the chair, taking his first breath in over a minute.

Jenna folds her hands in front of her face and opens her mouth to speak, but nothing comes out. Her eyes close and her smile fades.

"I didn't expect to leave you speechless," Matt kids.

"I'm not a quantum guru like you and," she hesitates, weighing the consequences, "your father, but are you considering whether the issue has a nonhuman, external source and may not be in the code?"

He's shocked to hear Jenna mention his father. Despite the length of time he has been gone, it's still very raw to him. Grief over his disappearance waits quietly in a corner of Matt's mind behind life's regular trauma, rolling over him when his thoughts drift. It's been a while since he has been reminded of it, and it takes steady concentration to keep it from knocking the wind from him.

Matt pauses, then replies. "Yes, everyone believed he was brilliant and able to solve challenges no one else on the planet could. If he were here, he would know what to do, where to look." Gathering himself, Matt locks eyes with Jenna and says, "You would have liked him."

"For sure, he was a once-in-a-lifetime talent, a first-generation success story. So much so he was able to work his way up the ladder within a caste system that 'didn't exist.' He solved many technical issues surrounding room-temperature quantum computer systems, and he kept his ego in check, unlike others around him," Jenna responds.

Matt chuckles. "Where did you read that? I must have missed that article. Truth is, he was pretty tough on me."

"He needed to be, raising you alone after your mother passed away, trying to live a lifestyle his peer group would approve of, beyond his means and the temptations that came along with it."

Matt's face turns red. "Wait a minute. You're talking as if you were friends with my father, my family." His jaw clenches. "And what are you implying about our lifestyle, about trouble he may have been in?"

Jenna puts her arm around Matt to comfort him. "I can see how hurt you are. Your father's disappearance is still an open wound. I'm sorry I have not been more present in your life to help you get through your pain."

"Thank you, but that's not your responsibility. My father operated in a sphere different from your academic life. There's nothing you could have done."

Jenna takes a deep breath, carefully weighing the possible outcomes of the next few minutes. She begins her confession. "Matt, it's time I tell you the truth about my relationship with your father, with Niera, and our work together. I'll let the chips lie where they fall afterward."

Matt stands and steps back to put distance between him and Jenna. He asks, "Who are you really, and what do you know?"

Jenna describes the close working relationship she had with Matt's father, John Boson, and Niera and how, twenty-five years prior, the three colleagues were the first to develop stable room-temperature quantum systems.

"Niera was the visionary and enjoyed the spotlight, your father the quantum engineer hiding in the shadows, while I provided the framework for integrating artificial intelligence learning into a quantum environment. Our success ushered in a wave of advancements in all disciplines; scientific, robotic, agriculture, and medicine, to name a few. For a long time, we did incredible things together. We were like-minded, and then something happened."

Eyeing her suspiciously, Matt says, "What, like keeping secrets from those around you, or lying by omission?"

"That's fair, but no. I can't put my finger on it exactly. Sometimes I think it was Niera's growing lust for power. Other times, I felt it was Drazen entering the scene, or even global forces trying to control our innovation? I guess it doesn't matter. What I want now is to be truthful and help you find closure with your father's disappearance."

Matt paces the room trying to mitigate the anger building up inside him. He begins shooting questions at

Jenna like she's a target. "You had this information when you met me in college. Why did you hide it from me? Was Alyssa aware?"

"No, and I've said nothing to her since."

"What happened to the intellectual property you created, and what caused the three of you to split up?"

"Let's just say we had a fatal disagreement about who should benefit from our work, and how far we should push our capabilities."

"What do you mean?"

"As part of the work I was leading, we pioneered a human replication algorithm. It used the power of quantum superposition to allow artificial intelligence programs to replicate human sentience, or at least it showed great promise in doing so. Niera pulled the plug on the research before we completed it, saying it was too dangerous. Drazen fought to keep it going but ultimately gave in. We archived our work, and no one has done anything with it since."

"That is a power that should not be in the hands of anyone with bad intentions. I'm glad it's gone. How did you decide to leave Niera and Drazen?"

"The excitement of our work together died out, at least for me, and after John disappeared, I felt at risk and came back to academia where it was safe."

Looking out the window, Matt asks, "When was the last time you saw my father?"

"It was a few months after the three of us split up. John came over and mentioned some trouble he was in. He didn't give me specifics but implied either Niera or Drazen was involved. It was important to him to have this part of his life behind him, to protect you from getting mixed up in it. And that is why I never told you. If I did, it would have opened a huge can of worms that I believed was closed for good. Seeing you today, I realize now how much of a mistake it was. I'm sorry."

"Did my father have anything else to say, something that can help me solve his disappearance? I'm aware of some of his weaknesses. I mean, it was not a secret he drank too much. I just don't see how that could have resulted in him disappearing."

"Nothing I can remember. His last words were to please keep an eye on you. I was suspicious of this comment knowing how close the two of you were, but he rushed out and I didn't speak with him again before he was gone."

The room is filled with a heavy silence. *I'm not sure I can trust her. She should have more information. There's something else she knows but is not telling me. This is a good start. I'm not sure how much more I can process, and besides, I need to change the subject and get the answers I came for.* "Despite our leadership's insistence, I ruled out hackers long ago and need innovative ideas. What did you mean by asking if I'm considering a nonhuman external event?"

Jenna smiles. "Your quantum world is so strange. There's someone much better suited to speak to about this."

Matt's eyebrows raise. "Who?"

"You know who. When was the last time you spoke?"

"If you mean Alyssa, it's been about eight years and forty days." Seconds later, he says, "But I could be wrong," attempting to show indifference.

"She's doing some amazing things now. Did you know that for two years after grad school she led NASA's initiative to place an array of space-based telescopes at the edge of our solar system."

"Yes."

"And, after being terminated for objecting to the United Nations' influence on the agency, she took her family inheritance and started her own space observation company while maintaining a part-time teaching role."

"Didn't she marry him?" Matt says with disgust.

"It was a speed bump and not relevant today. If you don't already know, Alyssa is just a short flight away in her Oregon teaching lab."

# 18

## THE PRESSURE

Five floors below Niera's office lies the company's brainstorming suite. The room carries a mystical reputation among employees, and everyone knows better than to show up unannounced. *Still, who wouldn't want the* CEO *to pay them a visit?* Niera finishes justifying the intrusion to herself as the elevator door opens. When she arrives, Drazen is at work.

Alerted to her arrival by the elevator's ding, Drazen saves and then erases the technical sketches he was analyzing. "To what do we owe the pleasure of this visit?" he asks.

"I need a friendly face." Niera says. "The calls and constant interruptions have me off balance, like I'm losing some control over myself. And the board's increasing pressure on me is confusing. It's as if they have inside information and are twisting it harder than I deserve. But why?"

Drazen stays quiet, waiting for Niera's next action.

She switches gears and begins meandering around the floor, looking at each detail like it was her first visit. "Seems like forever since I was here. Do you remember the early days when we would spend uncounted hours creating things to bring our vision to life? Now, we barely have time to think. How I miss the feeling of collaborating on the future."

Drazen replies, "Our plates are already overflowing, and much of what I'm working on would bore you to tears. Besides, you're far too valuable keeping the wolves at bay so the rest of us can do our jobs without interruptions."

Niera smiles. "It seems you're off doing your own thing most hours in the day. In reviewing your budgets, I see you have requested an exponential increase in the power costs for the data centers. Years ago, I would have collaborated with you on the projections. Today, I learn about things at the back end. Are you sure you have everything under control?"

"You can trust me. It's all going as planned," he replies. "Now let me show you something more positive."

Drazen launches a series of diagnostic tools and brings Niera around the table to show her the results. "More than ten billion hosts are active on the AIP. The new enhancements have convinced another billion people to join. Of course we will keep pushing the remaining population, but there will undoubtedly be a group of conspiracy theorists that stay away."

"This is great news. Now go tell Fitz he needs to do his job and find Boson."

"Why don't you tell him yourself?" Drazen says, pointing to the back of the room.

Confused, Niera turns around to see Fitz sitting alone in the corner. She whips back toward Drazen. "Why the hell didn't you tell me he was here? I could have said something confidential."

Fitz stands. "Ma'am, you would be surprised at what I know. I mean, a man in my position is paid to keep his pulse on the real action, to stay one step ahead...and to keep his mouth shut."

Drazen cuts him off, knowing Fitz is a loose cannon. "What he means is, we need to get ahead of the investigation into our system malfunctions."

Niera replies, "I agree, especially with the added pressure coming from the UN. So, Fitz, what is the good news surrounding what Boson has found?"

"I don't know."

Niera stares at Fitz, dumbfounded, before turning her gaze to Drazen. "Is this some kind of game? We don't pay him not to know. Get Boson's ass in here and I will ask him myself."

Fitz replies, "He's gone, ma'am."

"Gone? Now? Against my orders. Where did he go, and why?"

"I'm not sure of the why part, but we know he stopped for a period of time to visit someone at Berkeley."

"Berkeley," Niera says with suspicion. "The school has a lot of great engineering talent, so was Boson there to do interviews?"

"No, ma'am. It's something more...familiar."

Niera raises her voice. "I don't have time to call him right now. There's going to be hell to pay if he's plotting against me. Fitz, keep track of him. Let me know if he stops anywhere else. I'm going back to my office to take care of the wolves you mentioned earlier."

The elevator doors close behind Niera before Drazen approaches Fitz. "You know who is there and the risk it poses, don't you?"

"Yep."

"We cannot take any chances this late in the game. I need you to find out what they discussed, and I don't need to know how you get the information."

Fitz smiles, takes a final drink, and stumbles out knowing the gloves just came off.

# 19

## THE REUNION

Alyssa sits alone in her office two floors above the classroom where she finished her last lecture of the day. She's positioned on the wrong side of the desk, her back to the window in an effort to avoid being distracted by the beautiful landscape outside. Poring over satellite analysis and other data provided by Gaio, she doesn't notice the hole forming in her stockings, worn through by an hour of rubbing her knees on the desk's flat backside panel.

At the building's main entrance, Matt leaps up the last three steps, enters the lobby, and scans the directory. *Alyssa Starr, Room 310.* His knees shake as he approaches her door. He glances back at the stairs. *Am I really doing this? Breathe in through your nose and out through your mouth. She will be happy to see you.* He scans the hallway to assure himself he's alone and then peeks through the open slit at the bottom of the door's blinds. *I must look like a burglar making sure the coast is clear before picking the lock.*

He sees Alyssa and a wave of old feelings rises inside him. *She looks just like she did in her student apartment, cramming for a test while I stood outside the window, wondering if I should disturb her. Here goes nothing.* He gives a tenuous knock on the door.

Alyssa's eyes lift from the page, but she doesn't move. Her fingers tighten around the pen as she stares at the desk, willing herself not to look up.

"Nothing would make me happier than to ignore you right now." Her voice is edged with exhaustion, barely above a whisper.

She hears another knock and responds. "I'm sorry, office hours are canceled. Please reach out to one of the teaching assistants if you need help."

Matt grins and says in a loud voice, "My problems require someone with more tenure than a TA."

She drops the report. Her face lights up, and she tells the artificial office assistant to unlock the door. The handle turns, and the blinds bounce off the window as the door swings open.

She turns around slowly.

Their eyes meet.

Matt remains motionless.

Alyssa breaks the ice. "You must like it there in the hallway."

He responds, "With all your education, I'm surprised you don't know what side of the desk to sit on."

Alyssa rushes over but stops just short of where he

stands in the doorway. Their arms lift, hesitate, and then fall into an awkward hug.

"I see you're just as smooth as I remember you being," she remarks.

*Well, that was rather unsatisfying and anticlimactic after all these years,* Matt tells himself.

Alyssa steps back. "Matt, what are you doing here?"

Before he can answer, the sunlight cascades through the window behind Alyssa, creating a halo around her body.

Matt says, "You look...stunning!"

"And you look like you did after cramming all night for an exam."

"That bad, huh?"

"No, not at all. You're a welcome sight." She leans forward and gives him a kiss.

*That's better.* Matt pulls her close. "I really miss you."

"I know, me too, but..." She steps back and asks again, "What are you doing here?"

"I'm hoping you can tell me." Matt describes the issues around the world and the specific day and time they occurred. "Given the global reliance on GOD's computer infrastructure, this is a big issue impacting far more than the upper echelon of society. It's a challenge for the whole world, even though most people are blissfully unaware."

Alyssa responds. "There must be some higher power bringing you here after so many years without...even a phone call."

"That's snarky."

"I'm sorry, I didn't mean it that way. I know communication goes both ways. What I should have said is that it can't be a coincidence you show up only days after I spoke with the commander of an Icharus spaceship who described similar issues at the same time you mentioned."

"You must be right." Matt says. "There has to be a common cause."

"My artificial intelligence assistant used our telescopes to triangulate a potential source for the spaceship's issues."

"What did it come up with?"

"Well, we know what caused it and what comes next. Your reference to a big issue is orders of magnitude too light. Said another way, the big issue has not yet reached our world...but it will soon."

# 20

## THE INTERROGATION

Jenna arrives home to see a man's figure stretched out on her couch, bottle in his hand. She quietly backs up to the door and reaches for the handle, when she hears, "Leaving so soon?"

The familiar, yet unexpected, voice sends goose bumps crawling up her arms as she stands silent in the dark.

Fitz looks down at his half-empty glass, narrows his eyes, and mumbles, "Surprised to see me?"

Jenna does not reply.

"Don't worry, I didn't raid your liquor cabinet. I bought this from the corner store."

"I thought we all had an agreement. I would stay in my role at the university, and you would stay out of my life," she says.

"Isn't that a convenient statement from the person who is buddying up with Boson after all this time? A secret rendezvous of sorts?"

*How did he know about Matt's visit?* "We didn't talk about anything important."

"I'll decide about that. So, tell me, when did he contact you...to tell you he was coming?"

"He didn't. He just showed up on campus. Said he was in town and felt bad it had been so long since we connected. It was a short visit, and then he left."

"Did you make plans to see him again?"

"No."

"I'm sure it was a wonderful reunion. What else did you two old pals talk about?"

"Why is that a concern of yours?"

Fitz places the bottle on the coffee table and springs up. He inches closer to Jenna, his calm demeanor changes and his face hardens. "From this point forward, everything you talk about is my concern, everything you know is my concern, and everything you do is my concern. Do I make myself clear?"

Jenna steps around him and into the living room. "Stay away from me or I'll contact your handlers."

Fitz laughs. "You've been gone too long. The game is played by different rules now. Sometimes the dog chooses the direction on a walk."

*That makes no sense. He sounds more unstable than I remember.*

"Now, if you cooperate and you're truthful, I will walk out of here and it will be like I never showed up. If you're not...well, you know what's coming."

"I told you already, he was passing by and saying hi. I have no other information to give you."

After a long exhale, Fitz says, "If it were earlier in the

evening, I would enjoy going a few rounds with you, but I'm tired of this already."

Fitz lunges forward, pins Jenna against the wall, and places a mind-control collar around her neck. A few seconds later, his voice drops and he says calmly, "Okay, I kept this on low so we can have a conversation. Why was Boson here, and did he tell you anything about the Path Program or the Farm?"

Struggling to hold on to her wit, Jenna reminisces about her past work with Niera.

"I'm not interested in your history," Fitz yells. "I want to know what you and Boson discussed. Did he mention digital immortality?"

Jenna's face crinkles, and her head cocks toward the floor. She answers, "He mentioned problems he was having with his systems and that hackers were not the cause."

"What else?"

"He was having trouble figuring it out with traditional methods, so..."

"So what?" he asks, growing more impatient.

Jenna's words start to overlap, her voice alternating in volume and pitch. "I recommended he engage an old colleague."

"Who?" A drop of sweat drifts down Fitz's cheek as he becomes more irritated with the conversation. Taking a final swig from the bottle, he moves inches from Jenna's expressionless face. "Let's see how you react to this."

He intensifies the level of control over her thoughts. A smile confirms his enjoyment with the process.

Jenna's face goes blank as she collapses onto the couch. Fitz yells, "Oh no, not before I'm done with you."

He backs off the intensity. "One more time, who did you tell Boson to go see?"

Jenna struggles to identify where she is, to gain some element of control over her thoughts. The last thing she remembers before mentioning Alyssa Starr's name is the scent of cheap whiskey.

Fitz removes the device and comments, "Another example for the illusion of free will."

Moments later, Fitz exits through the front door, stopping on the sidewalk to be sure he turns in the right direction. On his way into the liquor store, he makes a call. "Hey, Architect, good news. They did not discuss the Path Program or the Farm."

"Don't call me that name on an open line. What's the next step?"

"I have a new lead to pursue. Alyssa Starr is about to make a new friend."

# 21

## THE FINAL ORDER

The Architect sits perched above rows of glowing workstations, watching cascades of symbols race across the screens below. Floor-to-ceiling concrete walls ensure sunlight is not used to distinguish night from day or to cause any distractions. It's an unneeded precaution considering everyone working is fitted with the latest mind-control device.

Glued to their chairs, they execute their tasks in silence, never questioning the purpose. They're allowed to leave only to use the bathroom, to get food, or to rest in one of the sleeping pods. Their sole source of communication comes from the Architect.

Directing the front row, the Architect says, "It's time to finish the features checklist for the adoption protocol." *It's hard to believe this is the most requested upgrade of the year, but to keep everyone happy, I must give the users what they want. Stupid fucking people!*

The Architect addresses the second row. "Finish

assessing the override protocols." No one flinches despite the obvious ethical challenges this creates.

For everyone else, the Architect says, "Once the override is confirmed, upload the beta subject's digital sentience, and report progress to me in real time."

A designer from the last row stands. "Upload complete. Parallel neuroactivity and decision observations between the host and the host's avatar commencing."

"Run the avatar through ninety minutes of experiences and report back on the percentage accuracy," the Architect demands.

At the ninety-minute mark, the Architect hears, "Three deviations per million."

"Not good enough," he yells back. "Where did we miss?"

"Duress decision-making and olfactory awareness," responds the designer.

"Deactivate the betas and get all rows to fix the issues." *We need to push the errors to under one per ten million or we cannot guarantee the accuracy for digital sentience demanded by the board.* "How long until it's fixed?"

"Less than forty-eight hours."

*So many years of work are ending. No, not an end but a beginning. Soon every host will have a choice: remain with the misery of their short-lived physical existence or opt into eternal happiness.*

A digital register activates behind the Architect. A smile fills his face as he sees the AIP has surpassed ten and a half billion hosts. *The game has been rigged...making this important milestone inevitable.*

Before giving his next order, the Architect notices a

loud clicking sound in the ceiling. *One of those blasted cooling fans is vibrating. I guess it's not a surprise given the heat this facility generates. We need over a hundred of them to stay cool. I'd have it fixed, but we will be done with this place soon.*

The Architect gives a final order. "Hide the global opt-in protocol inside the AIP. Use the avatar we previously discussed. We will be releasing it to the masses soon." *The countdown begins.*

# 22

## THE MISTAKE

Matt's sitting on the couch in Alyssa's office, his feet resting on the edge of the coffee table, and asks, "So, you believe the three data points are connected?"

Alyssa rolls her eyes. "Come on, Captain Obvious. It's too much of a coincidence if they're not. How could my space telescopes observe a relevant cosmic event near the same time the Daedalus spaceship is damaged and minutes later the GOD quantum systems on Earth are disrupted? And finally, the observations and disruptions stop in all three places without corrective actions on anyone's part."

Alyssa waits for a response. After a few seconds, she throws her arms up and yells, "Did you hear me? What are you thinking?"

"Why didn't your space telescopes suffer any damage from the gravitational wave? You must use quantum computers on each of them."

"I don't use the GOD quantum systems." She turns, hoping to avoid the natural follow-up question.

Matt smirks. "Why were you connected to the spacenaut? Do you know her?"

"No, Gaio called me. He wanted help..."

Matt aggressively cuts her off and says, "So your CEO husband came calling, looking for help, and you just bow down to him again trying to do what you can."

Alyssa responds calmly. "He's not my husband anymore, and I don't owe you any explanation on my choice in relationships."

"I know you don't, but now that we're on the subject, I'm curious what happened to the two of you."

"Let's just say we failed fast. We were star-crossed lovers, an astrophysicist and a rocket engineer. He used his fortune building spacecraft for future colonization of the solar system. It was one of the few industries independent from the reaches of your employer. It quickly consumed all his energy and attention."

"You're right, GOD focused mostly on Earthbound affairs, leaving an opportunity for those with eyes into space. I'm guessing that's why you chose to build your array of space-based telescopes away from the grip of GOD."

"I chose the more noble path of teaching and stargazing rather than chasing profits and influence. Now, I don't suspect your surprise visit is to ask about my career. How can I help you unravel your issues?"

Before Matt can respond, a loud knock sounds at the door. Alyssa instructs the office assistant. "Close the shades and lock the door."

A voice echoes from the hallway, "Ms. Starr, I see you in there."

"Office hours are canceled, and besides, I've seen you twice already this week," Alyssa responds back.

"Canceled? Your automated booking tool mentions nothing about canceled hours, and besides, there's someone in there already. Do you think I'm blind, or stupid?"

Alyssa looks at Matt and asks, "Do you think she wants me to answer that honestly? I mean, if there were a zombie apocalypse and they fed on brains, I'm sure she would survive."

Matt smirks and they ignore the student until she eventually walks away. He then discusses the uniformity of the quantum disruptions across the globe and adds, "What concerns me the most is that businesses and industries utilizing the advanced GOD quantum systems suffered the majority of issues."

"Are you saying all the news reports of failures and loss relate only to your clients?"

"Not all of them, but a statistically high-enough percentage to know we have an issue, and it's my ass on the line since I'm responsible for our quantum environment."

"What happened to businesses running on GOD's older technologies?" Alyssa inquires.

"That's the weird part; nothing. They're all fine. So, how could a hacking operation be successful against the most secure and sophisticated systems ever built but the old technology provides protection? I'm at a loss, nowhere else to turn, so I came to your doorstep looking for help from an old friend."

"A friend *and* old." She glares at him. "That's not going to buy you much around here."

"Oh crap, I guess I just put my foot in my mouth."

"I'm joking. I see you haven't outgrown your awkwardness. I suppose it's why you excel in a world of quantum uncertainty."

Matt looks down before continuing. "I should also tell you how I found you here."

"Yes, I was wondering that."

"I went to see Jenna for advice. She looked better than she did eight years ago, but her nurturing personality was missing. In fact, she opened a major wound I thought I had under control."

"I'm sorry." Alyssa says. "I haven't spoken to her in quite a while. What wound, and did she provide insight into your issues?"

*It's not the right time to get into my father's disappearance. Focus on the system issues first.* "She suggested it may have something to do with forces working well below the macro environment. What keeps coming to mind is some aspect of quantum entanglement."

"Entanglement has nothing to do with it. I place my money on something less spooky, something originating in the cosmos, specifically gravitational waves."

Matt responds, "You say that with a high degree of confidence. Gravitational waves in our solar system and the surrounding space shouldn't be significant enough. What do you know?"

"My telescope array came online days before an unexpected cosmic event was observed. We penetrated through what we believed to be a dense, innocuous cloud of hydrogen gas with trace amounts of other elements. We discovered something unsettling at the center...a pair of neutron stars in orbit around each other. This was surprising enough, but we also saw the orbital plane was rapidly deteriorating. In a nutshell, the neutron stars were on an inexorable path to collide. An initial, glancing blow created the gravitational wave we each experienced days ago."

Matt asks, "What do you mean by glancing blow?"

Alyssa continues. "This is a classic binary neutron star collapse. We modeled it out and know exactly what the next steps will be."

"Next steps?"

Suddenly, another student begins knocking at the door and wrestling with the handle. "Ms. Starr, are you in there?" a man asks.

"I wish these students were as committed to homework as they are to knocking down my door. Excuse me for a few minutes while I deal with his questions."

Alyssa steps into the hallway, closing the door behind her.

Matt gazes out the window at the educational complex below and high-rise buildings of the city center in the distance. *I don't feel I have control of anything. Our systems are under attack from invisible energy waves. There are hidden areas within the server environment I built qubit by qubit. Everything is in turmoil, and the problems are right under my nose. I need her computer. I need to show Alyssa firsthand.*

Matt activates Alyssa's three-dimensional display and launches a mid-level hacking protocol, easily cracking the institution's security protocols, and gaining full control over her system. Matt laughs. *Higher education obviously doesn't mean higher security.* Within minutes, he's navigating through GOD's main architecture but is stopped when trying to access the nonproduction servers.

Alyssa slams the door, looks back, and yells through the closed blinds, "Don't act like you caught us having sex on the desk!"

Matt turns and smiles. *Now that's a concept worth exploring in more detail.* For a moment, he forgets he was hacking into his employer's system.

Alyssa blushes, realizing her word choice was not the best way to encapsulate her hallway encounter. "I'm sorry."

"No need to apologize. I knew it was a crazy thought. The Alyssa Starr I know would never be caught in such a situation."

Alyssa chuckles, recalling that "on the desk" is exactly how it started with her and Gaio. She glances at the screen and realizes Matt is working with her computer. "What the hell are you doing?" she says. "My computer is part of the university infrastructure. I could lose my job if you're doing anything suspicious."

"I just need a few more minutes. I'm attempting an advanced hacking protocol."

"Hacking protocol? What do you have yourself involved in, and what are you pulling me into?"

"I don't know yet. I just need access."

Alyssa grabs Matt's arm and guides him toward the door. "Let's get out of here and finish our talk someplace more private."

Matt follows, forgetting to close the computer session.

The office door's automatic lock engages, and the words "Access Denied" reflect across the glass from the computer screen.

At the same moment back in his office at GOD, Drazen receives a warning message. "Nice try, now all I need is for you to stay open another minute and I'll know where to find you. Hmmmm, suspicions confirmed."

Drazen calls Fitz and says, "It seems Jenna was correct in naming Alyssa Starr."

"I'm just wrapping up here with Mrs. Grantham. Unfortunately, she's not looking too well." Fitz says with a smile.

Drazen replies, "Hurry, I need you to get Boson and Starr now. Bring them in using any method you deem necessary. I'm sending you their last coordinates."

# 23

## THE REALIZATION

Alyssa and Matt sit tightly against their respective doors as their autonomous cab pilots its way to Alyssa's condominium. Matt rests his head on the window, gazing outside at the structure of the city as the cab travels deeper into its center. Every large city is arranged the same way. Rural landscapes give way to low-rise housing, where most of the population lives. Moving closer, the mid-rise buildings reward the "useful" skilled workers, and finally, in the city center are high-rise luxury buildings for those who are either lucky, connected, or both.

The cab stops. Matt exits, looks at the top of the building, and steps back to catch his balance. He says, "That's a long way up in the clouds."

"I haven't noticed," Alyssa quips. "Now stay close. We need to clear the outside door's security." A series of marble steps lead up from the street. At the top is a large double-metal-door entrance between two large marble pillars. Alyssa leans forward, activating a retinal scanning terminal. A flashing green light precedes the click of the lock. The doors open into the main lobby.

Custom wood carvings and exquisite art pieces are elegantly positioned across the Calacatta Gold marble floors. A pair of two-sided fireplaces provide a warm glow to an otherwise-formal environment.

"One more checkpoint," Alyssa says with a smile. An oversized chandelier hangs above a polished metal desk positioned in front of the elevator bank.

Alyssa approaches the security station, where a humanoid asks her two security questions. A moment later, she hears, "Answers verified, and voice recognition confirmed. Welcome home, Ms. Starr. Please proceed to the elevator."

The doors open, and a man exits. "Good evening, Alyssa," he says.

"Good evening, Mr. Mayor," she replies.

As they get on the elevator, Matt glances over his shoulder. "You've got to be kidding."

"Be quiet," she says, jabbing her elbow into his side. "He's a long-term family friend."

Sixty dings later, Matt steps into a short hallway. He looks left and then right. "Are we on the right floor?" he asks. "Looks like there are only two doors."

From behind, he hears, "Turn right. It's unit 60-A."

"I was expecting at least a dozen units, given the size of the building."

Alyssa opens the door, allowing Matt to take a tentative step inside. Squinting to see the far end of her condominium, he says, "Stargazing must really pay off."

"I'm better at spending money than making it. This is all paid for with my inheritance. Apparently, Mom and Dad were savvy at navigating the system. Come into the living room, where we can be more comfortable and talk."

Matt asks, "You teach at a top university and own space-based telescopes. Surely those are lucrative?"

"Not really, my part-time teacher's salary barely pays for the wine I drink."

*Is she kidding with me now? She seems so different from when we were last together. And what's with this place? It looks like a bomb went off. Clearly, she has the funds to pay for a housekeeping robot.* "I see you've been working on your housekeeping skills since college. Piles of dirty clothes all around and yet you look photoshoot ready out in public. What's up?"

"Let's just say that my breakup left me with some holes that need tidying up. Now, not to change the subject intentionally, but in respect to my telescopes, I'm independent of the global order and disqualified from applying for lucrative government grants. I'll monetize my investments when I discover something extraordinary. Until then, it's a passion project."

"Something extraordinary, like...colliding neutron stars?"

"What a perfect segue, Matt." She smiles, her eyes twinkling.

A bright ray of light shines through the windows behind her, emphasizing the details of her face, the color of her hair, and her figure. *Something is different about her. She's more beautiful than I remember, as hard to believe as that is.*

"Matt. Matt," she says in a loud voice.

"Yes, what?"

"You're staring at me."

His eyes remain focused on Alyssa. "I was just looking at the gray streak in your hair and remembered how you thought it was distracting. I always told you it made you more beautiful."

He catches himself. "Right, sorry. In your office, you mentioned a glancing blow. Are there more to come?"

"Yes, but only one."

"At least tell me the first was the worst?" he asks, knowing the probable outcome.

Her grave look is the only answer he needs. She explains, "Based on the physics calculations, there are fourteen days between the initial collision and the final one. Earth experienced the first wave six days ago, so we have eight days until the second wave reaches us."

Matt hesitates and then asks, "How much stronger will the second gravitational wave be?"

"At least a thousand times."

Matt's face goes pale. "That could be devastating," he says, defeated.

Alyssa looks surprised. "Why are you so worried? Gravitational waves are a regular occurrence throughout the universe. No one will even feel it."

"From the perspective of twelve billion humans, you're correct. However, our quantum cages are designed based on assumptions of known gravitational events near Earth, with a buffer of course. We saw what happened with the first wave. Our qubits may not accommodate such a degree of gravitational wave fluctuation."

Alyssa responds, "Ten light-years isn't near Earth. It's sixty trillion miles away."

*I can't believe she hasn't put this together yet.* Matt winces and asks, "How much weaker will the waves be after traveling ten light-years through space?"

Alyssa replies, "Not enough."

"Exactly." Matt's thoughts of chaos in their servers around the world are interrupted by a call from Eugene. Pressing his temple, Matt hears, "Hey, boss, not sure what it means, but Fitz came down looking for you...said you were in trouble, something about an inside job."

"What did you tell him?"

"I don't know where you are, or what you're doing, so I told him the truth...nothing."

"Anything else he wanted?"

"Yeah, he wanted to know why you were at a teaching lab with someone named Alyssa Starr. He mumbled something about having a date with her soon and there would be a price to pay for visiting the Farm. Does any of this make sense?"

"Right now, nothing makes sense, Eugene. How are you and the team doing?"

"We're okay, but everyone would feel better if you were here. Fitz spooked a few of us."

"Tell everyone not to worry. Fitz is just being Fitz. I'm coming back tomorrow. Hang in there until then."

"Gotcha, boss, see you then."

Matt grabs Alyssa's shoulders. "If we're to get in front of this, you need to come to GOD with me."

"Are you crazy? I can't just leave. I have class, not to mention a looming catastrophe to investigate."

"That is exactly why I need your help. We need to convince Niera your catastrophe and my issues are intertwined. My father used to say everyone's life has at least one critical inflection point and people who recognize it, and then act on it, can take control of their future. I don't know how to convince you, but this is an inflection point for both of us. After all this time, science has drawn an intersecting path for our lives...forcing us into something bigger than we know. We must recognize it and work together."

Staring at the family pictures on the wall, Alyssa says, "My parents said something similar to me before they passed away. Honestly, it's part of the reason I pursued my own company, leaving the world's institutions behind."

In a demanding tone, Matt says, "Then you'll come with me?"

"If you had been this spontaneous ten years ago, we may have been something."

Matt's head drops.

"I'm sorry, Matt. I meant it as a joke," she says, already regretting the comment.

"None of this is a joke. I'm leaving, and I need you to trust me and come with me."

# 24

## THE CHAMBER

Drazen sits comfortably in the private residence of Niera's office, his hands carefully working a series of controllers on his lap. His choice of fine leather recliners bears contour marks from his frequent use.

Nearby, a nano-chamber hums as Niera approaches the end of her treatment. The sound stops and the door panel slides open. Niera steps out. A bright-blue hue shimmers behind her brown contacts.

Drazen stands and asks, "How are you feeling?"

Niera disconnects the cerebral cap and shakes off some instability. "Give me a few seconds." The blue hue disappears. She moves close to Drazen and demands, "I want the report on Boson's findings now."

"We don't have it yet."

"For God's sake, it's been a week. I suspect a team of monkeys would have been able to figure it out by now!"

"Welcome back, Niera. I see your sharp wit is not lost."

"Stop with the games, Drazen. Do I need to go to Boson myself?"

"No! Fitz and I have been on him to make this investigation a top priority. When I went looking for him this morning, I learned he had gone out of state in violation of your grounding orders."

"Remind me. Where the hell did he go?"

"Let's go to the conference room. Fitz is there and can shed some light on the situation."

Drazen follows Niera through a narrow back hallway and enters the conference room from a hidden door. Fitz is in his usual spot, standing guard over the drink cart at the back of the room.

Niera acknowledges Fitz but then directs her anger at Drazen. "Why can't you get me the answers I need?"

Fitz immediately chimes in. "Good afternoon, Niera. I visited Boson myself. Made it clear what's expected of him."

Niera snaps back, "You know as well as I those were hollow threats. It's not like he's an indentured servant. Perhaps your methods have lost their 'punch.'"

Fitz slams his glass on the table and steps toward Niera, his face red hot.

Drazen intervenes. "Step back and calm down, Fitz." Turning to Niera, he says, "You won't be as cavalier about his insubordination once you understand where he went."

"Oh yeah, where is that?"

"He left to pay a visit to his former graduate-school mentor, Jenna Zane. After their meeting, he reconnected with an old college fling. Fitz, show her the details."

Fitz weaves slowly through the room, making a

withdrawal from the drink cart before turning on the visual control panel.

Niera reacts. "So that is what he was doing at Berkeley."

"That's just the start," Fitz says, pulling up more of Alyssa's details. "This is her family, her education, her occupational history, and finally, her ex-husband. You know, ma'am, innocent people don't run to the enemy."

The information hits a nerve. Niera shouts, "This feels like corporate espionage. They could be trying to bring everything down, even our upcoming initiatives. Are they aware of the billions of people who will be affected?"

Drazen flashes a sly smile at Fitz...*job well done*.

Giving them both a cold glare, she directs, "Whatever you're doing to find them is not enough. Fitz, I want this to be your top priority. Engage the assets you're always bragging about and bring them to me within the next seventy-two hours!"

Little does she know that ship has already sailed.

# 25

## THE FARM

Farmer Johnson sits alone in the dark corner of his living room. He continues to scootch his chair just enough to remain beyond the streak of sunlight as it progresses from left to right throughout the day. The chair's original color faded away at least five years ago and is now as muted as the overall atmosphere inside the house. Johnson turns himself ever so slightly to keep his elbow on one of the remaining fragments of fabric hanging on the wooden armrest.

On this rare occasion, Johnson is not connected to the AIP. He finds himself reflecting on the past. *Do you remember what life was like before your addiction to this damn AIP?*

A distant memory surfaces, forcing a faint smile. *I think I should try. At least for the moment it feels right.*

He touches his temple, trying to connect with his granddaughter, but the attempt is blocked.

A single tear flows down his face as he enters his login

to the AIP. *I don't have anything to say anyway. The platform gives me purpose. And besides, I'm sure my granddaughter's avatar will be happy to talk to me.*

The tear rolls far enough to lubricate his wide grin. He experiences a salty taste as he engages the ARC. He fades into the digital world, once again escaping the bone-crushing loneliness and physical maladies of the real world.

Moments later, Johnson receives a note flashing inside his ARC. *They're thanking me for my participation as a beta tester in the Path Program and for my patriotism. Now they're asking if I would like to be a beta tester for the Farm. They must think I'm special.* He responds, "YES!"

# 26

## THE ANNOUNCEMENT

A large crowd gathers inside the lobby of the GOD headquarters near a banner announcing the upcoming rollout of an enhanced AIP. Niera stands behind a curtain, awaiting the signal to come out. Her assistant is giving her last-minute instructions, preparing her for the types of questions she may get from the press.

Drazen leans over to Niera and says, “Keep your answers general, and point to a positive future. Don’t let anyone back you into a corner in respect to the exponential power needs GOD has recently required.”

His statement draws an odd look from her.

The lights dim. Niera steps out from behind the curtain and positions herself at the podium. The spotlights illuminate. All attendees are focused directly on Niera. It’s a position she has been in a hundred times, and one she relishes.

She begins with a summary of the company’s

achievements, emphasizing how innovations within the lifestyle platform have brought pleasure to the masses and peace for society.

Niera says, "Today is not about the past but rather to look confidently to the future. I have gathered you here to announce a major new upgrade in our Augmented Individualism Platform. Let me use an analogy to describe the leap forward. It's like saying the Icharus spaceships are merely an upgrade on the Wright brothers' classic plane."

Questions come flying in from the crowd, all of which Niera disregards. She waits for a lull before continuing. "We've completed the integration for our patented Pentasense replication system and the bio-memory protocol. We can now capture, retain, and recall all memories for every host, and we can predict, or replicate, exactly how a host thinks and feels in any scenario. Life within the AIP can be as good as, if not better than, life outside it."

Drazen hands Niera a note card and says, "Read this verbatim."

Niera continues. "One final item," she reads from the card. "We sent out invitations to a select number of hosts to participate in a beta test for the new AIP and should have the results soon." She looks back at Drazen for clarification, but the reporter's overlapping questions distract her.

The first reporter asks, "Have you determined what caused the malfunction in your systems last week?"

"What have you done to assure the public this won't happen again?" someone else shouts.

Another reporter calls out one last question from the

back: “Do you worry that the AIP might be creating emotional or psychological dependence?”

Niera brushes off all the questions except the final one. She turns to Drazen. “What the hell gives him the right to ask that, in public? Find out where he’s from and make sure Fitz visits his editor. We cannot have the public questioning our methods.”

“Got it.”

“Also,” she says, “has Fitz intercepted Boson and Starr yet?”

“Not yet, but he has a hot lead and is en route.”

# 27

## THE HYPERLOOP

Matt and Alyssa arrive at the city's main rail transportation station. They stare at the contrast between the gleaning silver tubes of the high-speed hyperloop transports and the rusted-steel color of the legacy commuter tracks.

Alyssa hesitates as Matt tries to pull her along. "Let's go, we need to be on the next hyperloop transport back to Niera," he says, turning around to emphasize the point.

"Why do you want to go on a train when we could cut our travel time by flying?"

Matt barks back, "If the second wave hits, would you rather be in the air or on the ground?"

She shoots him a look. "It's not going to hit for several days. You should trust the science."

Passing through a series of security scanners, they take the up-ramp to the hyperloops. Stepping onto the platform, Matt stares at a group of passengers. *They're heading home with no idea of the potential danger coming their way.* "Ignorance is bliss," he whispers.

"What are you saying?" Alyssa asks.

"Nothing, just commenting on the time remaining until our transport arrives."

Alyssa spots a digital clock counting down while a red emergency-exit sign illuminates the platform behind them. "Five minutes to go," she announces. With no reply from Matt, she says, "Did you hear me?"

"Something is wrong," he responds. "There's a man approaching from our right, and it's one of Fitz's lieutenants. I suspect it's not a coincidence."

Alyssa scans the platform, her eyes widen. "Matt, six other men are coming up the platform, all wearing the same military gear."

Fitz's lieutenant, Brass, approaches the couple.

"What are you doing here, Brass?" Matt demands.

The lieutenant smiles slyly. "We're going to need you and your friend to come with us."

*How did they know where we were? Where are they planning to take us? This makes no sense!* Matt asks, "Why?"

"Surely you're aware of GOD's strict confidentiality clause...and I hope I'm not the first one to tell you who she has been sleeping with." He blows a kiss at Alyssa.

*I don't get it. None of our activities rise to the level of sending trained killers to apprehend us.* Matt replies, "We're on our way to see Niera right now, to provide her with valuable information. What do you think we've done anyway?"

Brass inches forward. "Does corporate espionage, spying, and accessing restricted sites ring a bell? You may eventually get to see Niera, but you have a date with someone else first."

Matt fires back at Brass, "I'm not accessing restricted sites. I have a responsibility to build and maintain all the company's systems, and besides, Niera demanded I do anything I needed to find a solution."

"You can tell yourself whatever you want. As for right now, you're coming of either your own volition or ours," he chirps, "and I hope it's the latter."

Matt sees one of the other men step forward holding a pair of horseshoe collars. "Why do you need those for us?"

The lieutenant responds. "Don't play games with me. Your recent activities are enough to convict you of high crimes. I'm reaching the end of my patience with you."

Matt looks at Brass, scratches his head, and says, "No pun intended, but it seems you're coming off the rails."

"We'll see once we have some playtime with your mind and Ms. Starr's."

Matt looks at Alyssa, seeing fear in her eyes. *The situation is more serious than I previously comprehended.* Matt cocks his head quickly in the direction of the red emergency-escape light hoping Alyssa will understand.

She nods to confirm.

Matt yells, "Are you really going to abduct us with a team of tech workers over there watching everything you are doing?"

Brass turns to gauge the situation and sees only his security team in the vicinity.

Matt shoves Brass backward into a trash receptacle, causing him to crash to the floor.

Alyssa reacts immediately and bolts for the emergency door, holding it open for Matt, who is a few steps behind her. A shot rings out, hitting the metal doorframe inches from Matt's head. Once through, they jam the door's handle with a fire extinguisher and run down the stairs.

Brass looks through the small glass window, losing them as the stairway turns in different directions. He hollers back at his team, "Go down both ramps and cover all the street exits."

Moments later, Matt and Alyssa come out between a series of active hyperloop guideways. Looking at the departure schedules for each train, Matt says, "Get into that hyperloop. It's scheduled to depart in less than two minutes, and give me your GLD."

"What? Why do you need my global link device?"

"I have an idea."

Alyssa carefully removes it from her ear canal and hands it to Matt. "You know I'm now disconnected from my artificial intelligence program and communication link to the world?"

Matt disregards her question. "Now, come closer. I need to take a picture of us sitting together."

"You have your priorities mixed up. We're not going on vacation. We need a plan to escape," she demands.

"That's what I'm doing." He takes the picture with her GLD, verbalizes a command, and places it on the seat. "Now, let's get off before it departs."

"What about my GLD?"

"Leave it and get on the next hyperloop. It's also leaving soon."

"I hope you know what you're doing, Matt."

Matt removes his GLD, takes another picture of them together, verbalizes another command, and places it on the seat. "Now, jump off and go to the commuter train tracks."

Behind them, each of the devices activate, projecting a hologram visual of them sitting together on each of the hyperloops.

Outside the train, Brass's men report seeing Matt and Alyssa together on two different transports.

"That's not possible," the lieutenant yells. "One of you must be mistaken. We don't have time to make another visual inspection. Split the men into two teams and get on both the hyperloops. Go now, before they depart."

The men enter the back car of the hyperloops and walk toward the front, where Matt and Alyssa were seen. The hyperloops depart and are far outside the city before the men reach the seats with the GLDs.

Brass receives the update from each team and smashes his fist on the table.

Inside the commuter train, Alyssa asks, "Why are people from your own company chasing us? We're trying to help them. Why are they threatening us?"

"It must be because of something I found."

"What?"

"I don't know."

Through pursed lips, she says, "It feels like my life is in danger because of you, and you're talking in circles. Can you get more clarity around what you found so we can work together to deal with it?"

"Not from here. I need a system with a lot of power."

Alyssa asks, "Then why did we get on a commuter train? It moves so slow."

"Because we need things to calm down before I can make another attempt to learn what we're up against. Traveling low-tech and leaving town makes it harder to be followed."

"Where is this train taking us?"

"To a remote ski village for the elites. No one will expect us to be there, and since they don't like their lives under surveillance, we won't be identified on camera."

"Funny how they built an infrastructure to monitor everything we do and program us to think what they want, but when it comes to the same for them, it's a no-go. What a bunch of hypocrites!"

"We will be at the village in a couple of hours. In the meantime, I've figured out how they are finding us, and I need you to help me with something."

"What else could you possibly need now?" Alyssa curtly replies.

Matt cringes and says, "We need to create a Farraday cage of sorts."

"You're still not making any sense."

"It will make sense in a minute." He pulls a small piece of gold foil from an air-purifying vent. "My security level requires I have a specialized locator chip implant. They say it's to help them locate me quickly if I'm taken hostage."

"How loving of them." Alyssa comments.

"Get behind me." He says.

With his head bent down and his ear folded over, Matt

asks, "Do you see the small red light glowing under my skin above my earlobe?"

"Yes."

"Okay. It's necessary to cover it with gold foil to prevent it from transmitting a signal."

"There must be another way. I mean, will this even work?"

"It's rudimentary, but it should at least cloud the signal until we can find a way to remove the unit entirely."

Alyssa places the foil over the back of Matt's ear.

Pointing to the wall, Matt says, "Now, I need you to remove the staples from the train's safety magazine and use them to secure the foil to my ear."

"Hmmmm, I have a better idea." Alyssa pulls out a piece of gum, chews it, spits it onto the back of the foil, and squishes it into the hair behind Matt's ear. She then rips a piece of cloth from her shirt and ties it around Matt's head.

"There. It might hurt a little to pull the gum from your hair later, but it's a lot better than shoving unsterilized staples into your ear."

"You always have my best interest at heart, thank you. Now, if you trust my motives, rest your head on me and let's get some sleep."

Seconds later, she moves closer.

A broad grin covers his face. *She feels like an angel on my chest.*

Alyssa hears, "We are going to have a challenging day tomorrow." Then, she drifts off to sleep.

# 28

## THE CABIN

Alyssa and Gaio are on another adventure high in the California mountains. They're nearing the peak on a trail unfamiliar to Alyssa when they reach a tight turn and drop-off. The view across the valley is as beautiful as the next few yards of the trail are ominous.

With her stomach pressing against the side of the mountain, she feels around the corner with her right foot. "I don't clearly see the trail, and I can't feel the ledge. I want to turn back," she says.

Gaio attempts to lift her fading courage but, unintentionally, only makes her feel inadequate once more. "Just step forward and search for the ledge with your foot. Don't let fear stop you...overcome the risk. I've done this myself, and I promise you'll be fine."

Taking Gaio's advice, Alyssa cautiously steps forward, clutching the rocks for support. Her right foot finds the edge, but her left foot skids off. As she tries to steady herself, her hands desperately reach out, finding nothing to grasp. She tumbles backward over the brink. Before closing her eyes, she glimpses Gaio turning around on the path above.

Just before she hits the ground, a hand catches her, lowering her softly to safety. Alyssa opens her eyes to see who saved her. It's the face of someone she hasn't seen since college.

Matt and Alyssa awaken to the screeching sound of metal-on-metal friction followed by a loud whistle, announcing their evening arrival into the mountain town.

Alyssa stares at Matt for several seconds, trying to reconcile her vivid dream with the reality of their situation.

"Now you're the one staring." He says.

Outside the train car, crowds move back and forth through the village square enjoying the last weeks of the ski season.

Alyssa yawns and says, "I could use a few more hours of sleep."

"Me too." Matt winks and says, "I guess that means I'm a comfortable pillow. Now, let's see how the elites live."

Stepping off the train, Alyssa asks, "Do you think the regular citizens know places like this exist?"

"Not unless it's on their avatar's vacation list," Matt jokes. "We need to get transportation and find some accommodations, preferably away from the crowds."

"What do you want me to do?" Alyssa asks.

"I'll get a rental vehicle, and since you have an oversized credit limit, you can get us warm jackets and a private cabin. Let's plan on meeting back here in thirty minutes." Matt crosses his fingers hoping there are no objections.

"I'm on it, but we'll need to use our credit accounts to make the purchases. Are you worried they will find us?" she asks.

"We don't have a choice, and besides, we will be gone by the morning."

Forty minutes later, Alyssa exits the tourism office and hears, "Your ride is here, madam."

She turns to see Matt on a snowmobile. "You sure know how to impress a girl."

"It's low-tech, with no communication links or tracking. Besides, tell me you're not excited about putting your arms around me to hold on."

"Like that night back in..." She stops herself.

After a twenty-minute ride up the mountain, they see the cabin. It's nestled between several mighty pines and has an air of serenity. The last vestige of the setting sun strikes the roof before retreating behind the western peaks.

Matt says, "This is perfect. We should be safe here."

As they settle in, Alyssa comments, "It's not an all-inclusive, but I did pay extra for a fully stocked kitchen. I'll open a bottle of wine if you get the fire started."

Matt gathers logs from a neatly stacked pile on the porch and looks around at the remote mountainside. He pinches himself to be sure it's not a dream. *I wish we were here together on vacation rather than hiding. Would she even want to be here with me? If we tried, we could make it together. That must sound crazy. We only reconnected a day ago. She should know. No more regrets!*

Alyssa settles into the trio of pillows at the end of the couch. "It's hard to believe this is all real. My life was moving along in a predictable way. It wasn't perfect, but I was happy and I was safe. Within just a couple of days, we're here, at the top of a mountain after escaping from people who were not wishing us happy travels. Where did those men want to take us, and why?"

"I can't say for sure. It became dangerous after I found the classified nonproduction servers and realized they were actually in production, hiding the Path Program, the Farm, and an opt-in protocol. Before that, people pressured me to find answers, but I was never threatened."

Alyssa leans back into the pillows and says with despair, "The Farm, the Path Program, opt-in protocols...what are you talking about, Matt? What are you involved in?"

"I wish I knew. It feels like I'm outside my body watching myself in a movie, unable to control the plot."

"Okay, let's start with an easier question. Who do you believe is behind the attempt to capture us earlier today?"

"They were Fitz's men, but he was not there. Niera has direct access to them and even Drazen, I suspect. In the end, I don't know for sure. I only know I'm sorry for getting you mixed up in it all. If I could go back in time, I would go home after visiting Jenna."

"I don't blame you, Matt. This is all very confusing, and your position at GOD means you have an entire world to protect. I'm sure you didn't have any other interest in looking for me."

Matt finishes his second glass of wine and flashes her a coy smile. "Truth is, I always wanted to look for you...to get back together, but not like this."

"You what?"

"I was unsure how to tell you at school, but I had strong feelings for you. I could never get my mind right. Too many feelings of loss from my mom's death and my father's disappearance to take the leap and tell you what I had felt for years."

Alyssa's eyes well up. "If you had real feelings for me, you would have found the courage to trust me, and I would have helped you through your pain."

"You don't understand. My emotional side was fighting my rational side, my heart screaming to tell you how I felt, afraid I may lose you. And just when I was about to talk, my brain shut it down to protect me from more hurt. In the end, I made the wrong choice and let you drift away without a fight. I have thought about that mistake over and over and will always regret not telling you the truth."

Alyssa stares at Matt for several seconds before opening another bottle of wine. "Would you like more?"

He grins. "Depends on how much of the truth you want to hear."

The glowing embers provide the main source of light in the cabin, and the sweet smell of burning oak hangs like a welcome haze in the air.

Across from the couch where Alyssa is sitting, Matt shuffles in his chair and asks, "Tell me about your husband. How did all of that go down?"

"My ex-husband! Looking back, it wasn't a relationship built on a solid foundation. It was more admiration and lust, in equal parts. He was older and brilliant, and I was just as much in awe of his intellect as I was in his ability to express his views in such a way as to have people agree and follow him like a soft cult leader. He also made no attempt to hide how much he wanted me, at least for a while. I got swept up in his storm. I tried to match his... how do I say it without adding a warning label...his sexual energy because it felt good at the beginning." Seeing Matt squirm, she asks, "Do you want me to continue?"

"Of course, I'm just repositioning. This chair isn't all that comfortable."

Alyssa asks, "Are you sure? Because your face looks like one of the burning embers in the fireplace."

"It's only because I'm sitting too close. I want to understand your story. Please go on."

Alyssa continues. "When my parents died, being an only child, I inherited their fortune and decided to pursue goals they would have been proud of; teaching and starting my own company. As I threw myself into work, Gaio fell out of lust, and I became less 'useful' to him. I was willing to try to make it work, but he had already conquered me, and when he realized I found something I admired as much as him, he called it off abruptly and left me searching for answers and in pain."

"I never met him, but I hate this guy already," Matt says, clenching his fists.

"He said he wanted to be friends. Can you believe the arrogance and narcissism in that statement? It ended as quickly as it started, and I needed to heal, to overcome the things he said to make me feel inadequate. So, I invested in a few 'physical' enhancements to boost my confidence while I worked on building a future for myself."

Matt stops her. "If you could see yourself through my eyes, you would know you don't need any enhancements.

Even the gray streak in your hair makes you natural, real, and more beautiful than any self-absorbed rocket man deserves."

"Thank you, Matt, but it was a short-term fix. Eventually, I realized the only thing I needed was to believe in myself and search for genuine feelings and people. There's not much more than that. How about you? Are you in a relationship now?"

"No, except that people tell me I'm married to my work, which is likely a true statement. At least with work as my spouse, there's no one to complain that I'm not home enough. Besides, there's only one girl I will ever love, and that was so many years ago." Matt shakes his head. *I can't believe I just said that. Why would I use a line from a Meatloaf song my grandfather listened to when I was young? I hope she didn't notice it. Time to change the subject.* "The fire is hot."

"Yes, it is. I may step outside a minute."

Matt stands up to adjust the fire, and Alyssa gets up to cool off. They find themselves very close. Emotion, danger, comfort, and wine all come together, and they kiss.

"That was nicer than I expected," Alyssa says with a smile.

Looking in her eyes, Matt affirms, "That was exactly what I always wanted."

She stares back at him, his touch and his eyes pulling from her feelings she has not had for years, her mind swirling with thoughts of their friendship at school and then the loss of trust in much of society and relationships. She makes a quick comparison. Matt's not like him. He's consistent, genuine, and his feelings for me have lasted through the years. He would never ask me to jump if I didn't see the ledge.

Matt kisses her again, touches her hand, and guides her willingly down the hall to the bedroom.

# 29

## THE ESCAPE

The snow on the long decline from the ridge to the cabin is undisturbed except for a single snow-boot trail. A rush of frigid air cascades down the mountainside like an avalanche, bearing down on Fitz. The smell of burning oak wafts across the sky as he pauses to assess the small stream of smoke coming from the chimney. *The fire is not being tended to. I may be able to surprise them.*

Fitz climbs the steps onto the porch, pressing his face to the living room window. He removes a small tool pouch from his backpack and, with the skill of a surgeon, cuts a small circular hole in the patio's sliding glass door. Reaching through, he flips the lock and enters the kitchen. Moving slowly as if he's walking underwater, he stops briefly to soak in the last moments of heat from the smoldering embers.

Staring down the hallway, he approaches the only room with a closed door. He turns the handle and peers in like an underaged patron at a peepshow. *Now, isn't this cozy?* He pulls a set of handcuffs from his back pocket and positions himself at Alyssa's side. He reaches, hesitates, and then with a quick motion, cuffs Alyssa's arm to the bedframe.

The clicking sound awakens them, revealing they're not alone.

Fitz smiles and says, "Surprised to see me? There's no place GOD can't find you, and by the look of things, you should be happy I didn't find you, say, two hours earlier." He winks at Matt.

Matt responds, "What are you doing here?"

"All in good time. Now, unless you want something bad to happen to your date, you need to come with me to the living room."

As Matt exits the room, he glances back to see a look of fear on Alyssa's face. He nods, trying to provide her with comfort before disappearing from her sight.

In the center of the room, Fitz grabs the open wine bottle, tips it back, and drinks like it's a cold beer on a hot day. Small tremors in his hands make it difficult to tie Matt's wrists to the coffee table. "Why are you collaborating with our enemy, and what did you do to the servers to cause our problems?" Fitz demands from Matt.

"You're drunk and crazy. I was doing the job Niera asked me to do. As head of security, you know I had to look at everything, even the secret servers." Matt waits a moment to measure any response from Fitz. Getting none, he follows up with, "You know, the ones needing a quantum key to unlock."

Unfazed, Fitz asks, "And when you were at the Farm, what did you see?"

Matt responds quickly, hoping to interrupt Fitz's line of questioning. "I'll let Niera decide how to handle it when I tell her what we've found."

"You found nothing," Fitz screams back at Matt. "The Architect is too smart for even you, my boy."

Matt's eyes curl inward. "Why are you calling Niera 'the Architect'?"

"I'm tired of this," Fitz growls. "You need more of an incentive to talk." He returns down the hallway to get Alyssa.

As Fitz slips out of view, Matt loosens the knots around his wrist.

Before uncuffing Alyssa from the bed, Fitz puts her in a mind-control collar and turns it on low. With Alyssa in a semiconscious state, Fitz returns with her to the living room.

"I'm going to give you a choice, Matt. Either you tell me the truth about what you know of the Path Program, or I turn up the power, and she becomes a new vegetable for the Farm."

Matt positions his body so Fitz can't see his hands are free. Trying to rattle him, Matt replies, "The Path Program is a covert operation to destabilize GOD's infrastructure so you and Drazen can wrestle control of the company from Niera, and I'm going to expose you!"

*He knows nothing that can hurt us yet. Now, what to do with them?* "Good try, Mr. Boson. We both know you have not found your way in, and you're grasping for straws." Fitz glances at Alyssa and licks his lips. "I wonder what she knows. I'll take her back to the bedroom and take a little peek like you did earlier."

Matt explodes toward Fitz with the tenacity of a rabid dog, knocking him over the couch.

Unable to help, Alyssa watches in terror.

Fitz shakes off the hit and stands up. "I didn't expect that from you, Boson. I'm going to enjoy pounding you to a pulp and, when done, I'm going to have so much fun with you." He turns his head toward Alyssa.

Matt reaches behind him, grabs a fireplace tool, and slams it into Fitz's cheek. Fitz lets out an unnatural roar and falls to the floor unconscious, blood oozing from his face. Matt, jaw clenched, ties Fitz's arms tightly to a log beam, saying, "I'm not taking any chances with you."

Alyssa points to the controller on the couch. Matt turns it off and pulls the collar from Alyssa's neck. A moment later, she regains control and embraces Matt. "Thank you for saving me from that monster."

Her touch calms his shaking. "I've never been in a real fight before."

"You were amazing."

Matt's eyes pop open and he pulls back. "We must figure out what's so important about the Path Program and the Farm that Fitz is willing to kill us to protect it."

Alyssa points at Fitz. "You really messed up his good cheek. What do we do with him, and what is your plan for us to escape?"

"We don't know how long he'll be unconscious, and I doubt he will cooperate with us anyway. Let's tie him to one of the cabin's wood beams. It's still before dawn, and if we hurry, we can get far away before he frees himself and contacts his network."

Staring at the white mountainside, Alyssa mutters,

"Far away...is that the best plan you have? I'm sure we will be safe if only we could get 'far away.' I don't think these people are going to stop until we're dead. I let my guard down with you, and the alcohol made me vulnerable. Why did I ever trust you again and let you lead me into this nightmare?!"

"Ouch," gasps Matt. "I didn't want any of this. It's not in my DNA to be taking on these people, and I certainly didn't want you to be in danger."

"I'm sorry, I know you didn't," Alyssa says, turning to look at Matt. "My life has flipped one hundred eighty degrees in a few days, and for what? We don't even know what we're trying to solve. I want to go back, but I can't... so I have no choice but to help you with Fitz."

"I'll get to the bottom of this, but I need to find a system with enough computing power to break through GOD's security, and I don't know where that will be."

Alyssa's eyes flash and she says, "I do. We need to catch the morning flight and visit my ex at Daedalus."

# 30

## THE UPDATE

Thirty people sit impatiently around a large meeting-room table. United Nations symbols fill the walls behind them. There are no name tags, and pleasant banter between the participants indicates everyone is familiar with each other. Background talk fills the room until Niera and Drazen enter, taking their places at the head of the horseshoe-shaped table.

Niera takes a deep breath and begins. "We've been making steady progress on our host registration goals and fully expect the newly announced platform enhancements will tip the scales with enough holdouts to quell any of your remaining fears."

A participant chimes in. "It's more than just hosts, Niera. We need confirmation that the compliance learning tools are working, our security is assured, and our replacement therapy is on track."

Niera calmly responds. "We will have no issues. The latest upgrade is our strongest ever."

Another participant interrupts Niera. "With all due respect, Madame CEO, your company has recently suffered a series of global system failures, and my understanding is that you do not yet know how they occurred. It seems to many of us you have a blind spot, and we're not going to accept anything other than complete success. The end is near and we want what has been promised to us."

Niera stands up, looking confused. "The end...what nonsense is this?"

Drazen cuts her off and addresses the group. "Let's all calm down and remember the scope of this meeting. Niera has done a stellar job building the platform and creating messaging tools for the hosts. As for other plans, I assure you I have control, and we won't fail. Our best people are working on the problems now."

Niera, confused, holds her hands open looking for clarity from Drazen.

"We want what has been promised to us," the participant yells again.

Drazen slams his fists on the table and says, "Everyone will soon be getting what they deserve." He grabs Niera's hand and rushes her out of the room.

# 31

## THE DAEDALUS CORPORATION

Matt and Alyssa emerge from the airport and catch a shuttle to the headquarters of Daedalus Space Exploration Corporation located outside of Austin, Texas. As one of the world's largest independent companies, it's a sprawling complex with huge manufacturing hangars surrounding outdoor spacenaut training fields and planetary surface reconstruction sets. At the center is a million-square-foot office facility.

Matt's eyes open wide, taking in the immense scale of the operations. He asks Alyssa, "And you were married to the guy who owns all of this?"

"It wasn't my focus when we were together. I wanted something more than a grand business venture."

*Yeah, I know what you wanted from him. You made that very clear last night.* Matt smartly decides to keep this thought to himself.

The perimeter of the complex resembles an old western fort; however, instead of a wooden outer barrier,

Daedalus employs retractable steel posts that stand eight feet tall. Alyssa and Matt approach the main security entrance comprised of an unimposing guardhouse and a narrow, two-lane road into the complex.

A human guard rests comfortably on her chair while a security humanoid greets them. "Can I help you?" it asks.

Alyssa steps forward and responds, "We need to speak to Gaio Estrella."

The humanoid intercepts Alyssa and asks, "Do you have an appointment?"

"No, but it's a matter of utmost importance, and if you tell him who I am, he will allow me in." She speaks in an elevated tone, hoping to be heard by the human in the guardhouse.

The woman looks up and says, "0713, return to neutral position." She steps out of the guardhouse and into the road. "Tell me what is so important and I'll check in with him."

"I can't, but I assure you he will want to see me."

"Oh, I'm sure he will. No one has ever tried using that line before," she says, smiling, and then turns to look at Matt. "And what about the drifter? Does Mr. Estrella want to see him and the wad of gum in his hair too?"

"He may not look like much, but under the hood, he has a lot to offer," Alyssa boasts.

Matt smirks and says, "This is Gaio's ex-wife, and I work for the GOD Corporation. Please reach out to his assistant and ask if we're welcome."

The guard takes a moment and then asks, "0713, did you sense any weapons or chemicals?"

"No, ma'am."

"Okay, the two of you, wait here."

"This seems to be going well," Matt kids.

He overhears the guard giving a detailed description of Alyssa's appearance, and then the guard says, "Yes, there is a gray streak on her left side."

Moments later, the steel crash posts retract below the road's surface. The guard waves her hand forward, saying, "Go to the main courtyard and wait. Someone will meet you there shortly."

"Thank you," Alyssa replies and turns to Matt. "Now let's move."

The walk to the courtyard is longer than Matt expects, weaving through buildings and people on narrow paths. By the time they reach their destination, he's filled with anxiety. Matt stares in awe at the massive buildings, wondering if they contain the equipment that could help him solve the issues. Just then, the cloud cover dissipates, and the sunlight illuminates the courtyard.

Gaio opens a door and crosses the manicured garden toward where Alyssa and Matt are waiting. His sandy hair and dark, bushy eyebrows accentuate his light-green eyes. A few days' stubble makes his squared-off face look more rugged, and his confident walk makes Matt insecure before the first words are spoken. *Geez, his clothes are more perfectly pressed than hers.*

Gaio gives Alyssa a long hug before saying, "I'm shocked to see you here. I thought you hated this part of my life."

"'Hate' is a strong word. Admiration at a distance would be a better way of describing our story."

"Fair enough. I'm very happy to see you."

"You don't look a day older than when we...uh, separated," she says with one eye raised. "I mean, you look great."

Gaio pivots toward Matt. "And who is this interesting character?" he says, offering his hand to welcome him.

With the sun behind them, Matt notices Gaio's shadow is several inches longer and thinner than his own. He tightens his stomach and breathes in to narrow the difference before returning the handshake.

Matt begins to speak, but Alyssa interrupts him. "To answer fully would take a lot longer than we have time for. What you need to know is that Matt heads up quantum computing for GOD and we go as far back as college. We shared a mentor. Someone you know, Jenna Zane. She reconnected us hoping we can solve the issues you and I talked about last Saturday."

Jenna's name causes Gaio's back to straighten.

Gaio gives Matt a curious glance. "I suspect we will learn a lot about each other soon. But before we delve into our stories, I imagine at least part of the reason you're here is curiosity about this complex. Let me show you what we've built."

The three hop into a pilotless helicopter and Gaio describes the facility from the air.

"This is impressive," Matt comments. "Did you plan it after the Drax Corporation from the old classic James Bond movie *Moonraker*?"

"Stop being a nerd...it's not helping," Alyssa mouths to him.

They land at the head of a football-field-size mound of grass. Gaio looks at Matt. "As accomplished as you have become in the industry, I thought you would be interested in where I house my quantum computer facility. It's here, belowground, shielded by one hundred feet of earth and steel. It would take massive force to damage this structure."

*I didn't expect him to pay me such a nice compliment.* Matt then asks, "Can you describe what issues you had with your quantum systems several days ago?"

Gaio responds, "With the exception of our interplanetary spacecraft, we had no issues."

Matt steps onto the grass. *I'd love to see what his facilities look like down there.* Turning back to Gaio. "Why only your spacecraft? The GOD infrastructure experienced disruptions around the world, so why would your operations be any different?"

"I can't be certain, but we develop and use our own proprietary quantum systems for every aspect of operations other than the interplanetary spacecraft."

"Why exclude the spacecraft?" Alyssa asks.

"I decided to be careful, to play nice in the sandbox with powers I don't fully understand. I agreed to use GOD's quantum systems aboard my interplanetary craft as a bit of a peace offering. I don't like the globalist powers, but I also don't want to be in conflict with them. I suspect it's not a coincidence the spacecraft had irregularities."

Matt's thoughts drift. *There must be some connection. We've ruled out hackers, and it's not statistically possible random events impacted only our systems...the best in the world. Wait, what if someone has been playing around with our safeguards to scale faster and cheaper. Is the Path Program a way to keep it hidden from my team? What has she been doing?*

"Matt," Alyssa says.

There's no reply.

Alyssa raises her voice. "Earth to Matt." She shakes his shoulder. "You need to snap out of whatever trance you're in."

Matt's face hardens. "Alyssa, we must ask him now!"

Matt turns to Gaio. "I need access to your most powerful quantum computer."

"Anything else?" Gaio responds sarcastically.

Alyssa steps in and says, "You must know we didn't come here by chance."

"I suspected such," Gaio responds.

She continues. "We're being pursued by individuals within the GOD corporation for a crime we don't understand. At the same time, we believe Earth is facing a human catastrophe from within and, as you know, a cosmic catastrophe from above."

"So you need me again," Gaio says playfully. "That has interesting connotations."

Matt's jaw clenches, waiting for Alyssa to put Gaio in his place. A moment later, he says, "Alyssa needs nothing from you. What I need is access to a system with advanced quantum tools and nearly unlimited computing power. Have you and your company been oversold? Is this too much to handle?"

"Hmmmm." Gaio scratches his head. "This is all very heavy. Follow me to the main building and fill me in on more of the details."

"How disgusting to watch you flirting with him after all you told me about your relationship," Matt says to Alyssa before moving.

Alyssa shakes her head. "What are you talking about? I was trying to help our cause."

"Oh yeah, by undressing him with your eyes."

"Matt, you're being ridiculous."

"We'll see. Maybe you and wonder boy should work together or even score another notch in the mile-high club on that fancy autonomous helicopter."

Alyssa steps ahead quickly and turns to face Matt. "Don't you ever say anything like that to me again. I trusted you, confided in you, even slept with you. I see you for who you are, and you owe me the same level of respect. Are you so fragile or dense you can't put that together?"

Matt shrinks and closes his eyes before responding. "I'm sorry, Alyssa. I haven't needed anyone for a long time, and I felt I was vulnerable to a ghost from your past. You're not just a number to me. I need to learn how to allow these feelings back into my life."

"I'll help you with that," she says, smiling. "Now, let's catch up to that jackass!"

Once inside, Matt explains to Gaio the extent of the system failures, being targeted immediately after discovering the secret servers, and their fortunate escape at the cabin.

After a series of questions, Gaio places his hand on Matt's shoulder. "It may surprise you, but I believe you, and will help where I can. I also like the idea of sticking it to GOD and its narcissistic leader. What specifically can I do?"

Matt says, "To start, I need a system that will allow me

to execute quantum hacking protocols with reverse encryption walls to keep us shielded from discovery."

"That is going to require an introduction to my second-in-command, Megan." Gaio's virtual assistant makes a call. Shortly after, a woman in her late twenties enters his office.

Alyssa catches Matt's double take, sneers, and says to Matt, "Now who is undressing someone with their eyes?"

"Not at all...uh, I was looking at the chart of elements sticking out of her pocket." *What a stupid thing to say, given exactly where her pocket is placed.*

"Yeah, and I was born yesterday. Keep your eyes on the objective," Alyssa responds.

After introducing Megan, Gaio tells her, "These are old friends of mine working on something important to all of us. I want you to provide them one hundred percent of your support."

Megan replies, "You know the Heisenberg uncertainty principle does not allow anything to be one hundred percent."

Still glaring at Matt, Alyssa blurts out, "Great, she's a female version of you."

*Is it possible...is she jealous? I like it.*

Gaio laughs but quickly returns to matters at hand. "It's not great timing, but I need to be at one of my other locations for the next two days and must leave you with Megan for now."

Alyssa responds, "But we need you here."

"No, we don't," Matt replies.

Gaio continues. "I had no idea you would show up at my doorstep, and there are things to which I'm already committed. But you're in great hands, and I'm only a call away if anything comes up. I have no other options."

Alyssa's head drops as Gaio exits.

Megan breaks the awkward silence by asking, "Where do you want to start?"

Matt says, "First things first. Do you have a medical facility?"

"Of course."

"Great, I need you to remove something."

Megan looks at Alyssa and asks, "What is he talking about?"

A few minutes later, Megan leads them to the medical office, where a scalpel-wielding robot removes the implant behind Matt's ear.

# 32

## THE CAT AND MOUSE

Megan brings Matt and Alyssa through several security checkpoints before reaching the end of a hallway and a set of sliding doors.

Alyssa asks, "Where is this elevator taking us?"

Megan smiles and says, "It's not an elevator."

Alyssa argues, "It must be. We're at ground level, and Gaio told us the computer facility is one hundred feet belowground."

"That is correct, but the medical facility is in the main office complex a quarter mile north of the computer lab."

"So?"

"So, we're getting in an inclinator, not an elevator. Elevators go up and down, and we need to go down and over at the same time. Gaio built inclinators to move at angles as they descend. Saves everyone time getting where they need to go."

"No surprise, he's brilliant," Alyssa comments.

Matt looks up. *Give me a break. I build quantum systems*

*that control the whole world's supply chain, and this guy builds a pulley that goes in two directions, and he's brilliant?* "Can't wait to see if he has thought of moving sidewalks."

"What did you say? I didn't quite hear you," Megan says.

"Nothing important. I'm just anxious to get to the lab."

The inclinator doors open. The team steps out into a small rotunda. Megan leads them a short distance through a concrete hallway to a closed set of doors. A banner above reads "Quantum Computer Lab."

As they step through the doors, Matt slows, he scans the dimly lit room and notices the less than state-of-the-art equipment. "I was expecting something more impressive from Gaio and the Daedalus Corporation," he groans, frowning slightly. This looks more like my grandparents' high school computer lab."

"Just wait," Megan mutters. "This is the private work area for Gaio, so its initial appearance is intentional. However, it comes with a few hidden enhancements for security." She then gives the verbal command, "Optimize."

Matt and Alyssa watch as the floor and walls begin a rhythmic motion with each section moving at a different beat. The floor is systematically replaced with an operating platform, while the walls are converted into video screens and panels.

"Impressive. What's behind those panels?" Alyssa asks.

"Dedicated quantum servers so nothing done in this room can be intercepted from the outside. Everything is voice activated and represented with three-dimensional outputs."

"Very cool," Matt adds with a grin.

"Now that we're ready, what would you like to do, Matt?"

"Does the voice recognition work for me?"

"Yes, you have been authorized."

Working from the primary operating platform, Matt instructs the AI to launch his remote access protocol using his personal security clearance.

"I'm in," he says.

Activating a custom backdoor key, he begins digging through the server architecture. Illuminated screens throughout the lab reveal the intricate structure of the system. Matt navigates to the Path Program and the Farm locations.

"This is where I always get stuck," he says.

Back at the GOD offices, Fitz sits in front of a screen sipping a pint of whiskey when Drazen comes in and asks, "Where did you get the matching scar on your cheek?"

"Very funny. It's a debt that will soon be repaid in full, with interest."

A soft ping causes Fitz to crack a smile, which, for a moment, connects with both scars, making his face resemble a villain in the old Batman movies.

Fitz leaps to his feet. "He's so predictable, couldn't resist using his old security clearance. Now that I have his location, I'll shut him down so he cannot discover anything else."

"Wait," Drazen says, "before you do that, give me the controls. I want to play a game with him."

"Why the hell would you do that?" Fitz yells. "Can't you see he's getting close to finding things we don't want him to see? Shut him down!"

Drazen fires back, "I have him right where I want him. I can picture him now, patting himself on the back, puffing out his chest for his new girlfriend, and boasting about how smart he is. Niera always says he's smart but insecure."

Fitz snaps. "I don't give a shit about your ego. You need to wake up. Right now, it's like the Ottoman Empire outside of Constantinople in 1453 CE. We're one cannonball away from him penetrating the outer wall."

"He will never break my firewalls, and I won't let him go until I teach him a lesson. Let's play a little cat and mouse, Mr. Boson."

Fitz makes a final plea. "This is stupid. Your intellectual superiority complex will endanger all of our plans."

Drazen brushes off Fitz's concerns and uses a voice scrambler to open a communication link directly with Matt. "I can see you knocking at the door of my Farm. What are you hoping to find?"

Matt lurches forward in his chair, taking the bait. "Who are you?"

Drazen responds. "Wouldn't it be convenient for me to tell you? No, you need to figure that out on your own. For now, you can call me the Architect, the person who built these beautiful programs right under your nose."

"What do you intend to do with them?" Matt asks. "They're housed in nonproduction servers, and they're using too much power to be kept secret for long."

"Here is a hint," Drazen teases. "It's a prison where everyone you love is going to be trapped."

"Love…you must not know me too well."

"I know enough about you, and I have been hiding in plain sight. It really came too easily."

Alyssa leans toward Matt. "I have an idea. This guy has a screw loose and huge ego issues. You may be able to exploit his overconfidence. Challenge him directly and see how he reacts."

Matt nods. "It's just a matter of time before I know exactly who you are and what you intend to do with the Path Program and the Farm. Once I have it, I'll…"

Drazen screams, "You'll do nothing. I have allowed you to get where you are now, and I control what you can do next."

Matt senses a change in momentum. "What I'm going to do next is bring you down a few notches." He launches a series of surprise malware programs to take control of Drazen's system.

Turning to Alyssa, Matt says, "If I can get control of his security settings, I can use it to allow me to breach the Path Program and the Farm."

Drazen's scrambled voice shrills as he intercepts Matt's malware programs. "You won't trick me with your petty resourcefulness. Others above you have tried and failed as well."

Confused, Matt asks, "Above me? Have you engaged with Drazen or Niera?"

Fitz wraps his hand tightly around Drazen's arm. "Get control of yourself." He demands.

Drazen takes a deep breath. "There's very little time left, and you will never break my PQC encryption."

Fitz shakes Drazen again. "Stop talking to him. We're burning valuable time."

Drazen's shoulders slump, and he says, "I have no intention of discussing this any longer with you. Goodbye, Mr. Boson." The screen goes dark.

Fitz grunts, and then a lopsided grin forms across his face. "It's not all unwelcome news. He was on long enough for us to get an exact hit on his location, but it's too far away for me to go personally. I'm going to scramble the reserves."

Handpicked and equipped by Fitz, a team of hosts from around Texas become activated mercenaries, their minds and bodies hijacked. Fitz downloads Matt's coordinates, sending the mercenaries out toward Daedalus.

"Make sure to bring them in alive." Fitz instructs the group. "I want to see their faces as the world collapses in front of them."

# 33

## THE MESSAGE

Matt's eyes widen as he gives Alyssa a hug. "Your idea to make him mad was brilliant. I now have an idea to break his encryption."

"I'm happy, but it sounded like a lot of boastful nothing. What specifically did you learn?" She asks.

"He said 'PQC,' which means it's a post quantum cryptography encryption tool. It's theoretically unbreakable, but in my role, I reverse engineered hundreds of the most sophisticated quantum hacking programs, many of them sent to me directly from Fitz. Over time, I covertly created powerful tools, and I never shared them with Niera, Drazen, Fitz, or anyone. I didn't trust how they would be used, so I hid them outside of the GOD systems, in my personal archives."

Matt turns to Megan. "Let's see how good your homegrown quantum systems are. If I'm going to break in, I'll need everything you have."

Megan steps away, makes a call, and reports back to

Matt. "You're in luck. After the issues with Icharus 9, we put a stop on the remaining scheduled launches this week. Other than routine operations, the systems are available for our use."

Alyssa and Megan watch as Matt uses the Daedalus quantum computers to attack. Every microsecond, hundreds of billions of attempts are made. Thousands of qubits in various stages of quantum uncertainty probe for the one acceptable solution to the PQC encryption lock.

After an hour and quintillions of coordinated attacks, Matt yells, "We're in."

Matt examines the design architecture, uncovering links between the Path Program, the Farm, and the new AIP rollout. *Its design is brilliant.*

With a mixture of disbelief and awe, Matt says, "We're dealing with a globally connected quantum brain, the largest I've ever seen. It's near infinite," he says. "I can't believe this has been built and operated under my nose." *The resources needed to run these two programs are five times what my team uses. Is this why I'm not allowed access to energy usage reports? Drazen and Niera must scrub them, allocating costs to other projects before disclosing them in their public reporting.*

Matt feels Alyssa's hand on his shoulder.

She says, "It's not your fault. Everyone has been deceived. This plan has been carefully shrouded by well-crafted words on a teleprompter, spoken by an executive with a sharp tongue."

"Yes, but..."

"But nothing. Looking into the sun will blind anyone."

Megan chimes in. "I'm not one to disrupt a good

therapy session, but we need to know more about the Path Program and the Farm. What does the code tell you about the operation?"

Matt responds, "It would take too long to reverse-engineer the code and give you a full answer, but at a high level, there are three main elements.

"The first is called the Path Program. It secretly extracts data from the AIP of every host, over time building a predictive map of each host's actions and emotions...essentially creating a digital, sentient replica of the host. That replica is then embedded in a duplicate avatar stored on hidden, nonproduction servers.

"At the same time, the system sends messages back to the hosts, encouraging them to accept an invitation at some point in the future."

"What is the invitation for?" Alyssa asks.

"Well, that leads to the second element. The invitation content is not in production, so I don't know exactly what it says. I can only see that, in order for the Path Program to 'activate and transfer' a host, the host needs to accept the invitation. After acceptance, they will be allowed to opt in, and the opt-in protocol will come from within the AIP."

"When will the invitations be sent out?" Megan asks.

Matt says, "I'm not sure, but it will go to billions of hosts at exactly the same time."

"Okay, let's play this out," Alyssa says. "What happens to a host after they opt in?"

"And that brings us to the third element: the Farm. It contains a cache and a mechanism to activate the host's sentient avatar once they have opted in."

Matt finishes his explanation by mentioning a raccoon trap at the Farm.

Alyssa tilts her head and says, "I'm following most of what you're saying, but a raccoon trap, what is that?"

Megan blurts out, "It's a one-way door that gets triggered after a host opts in. This may sound crazy, but once at the Farm, hosts have no way to get out. They remain in a digital state."

Alyssa is shocked. "What do you mean they remain in a digital state?"

Matt says, "It's a 'Hotel California' situation...you can enter, but you can never leave." *This is the second time I used a reference from one of my grandfather's old songs. She must think I'm a dork.*

A cold sweat forms on Alyssa's forehead. "Why would a host agree to be locked into a digital existence? What about their physical body?"

Matt continues. "That's an additional feature of the Farm, but I don't see exactly how yet."

Megan asks, "Is there anything in there to describe why they want to do this?"

"The program's output code suggests its objective is to boost plant and ocean production while reducing future demand on Earth's resources."

Matt pauses, studying the files. "There's also a reference to future safety, whatever that means."

Megan looks at Matt, "How many people are actively using the AIP? And more importantly, who are they exactly?"

Matt presses his hands over his face, the realization of the answer hitting him all at once. "There's no way this can be happening. The hosts are primarily the helpless masses across the globe."

Alyssa says in despair, "So the Path Program is meant to digitally replicate a host, trap them in a digital existence, and send their bodies to the Farm? That's George Orwell stuff. No one would ever do something like that."

"Under any other circumstance, I would agree," Matt says. "But look at what they're doing to us. They're willing to kill us to protect their plans. If we move past the initial shock, and if we are honest with ourselves, don't we all have questions about the influence exerted on individuals' autonomy as they become more addicted to the AIP?"

"Yes, but who would intentionally do this?" Alyssa sighs. "It must be someone with a lot of resources."

"I suspect you are right." Matt replies. *I've worked with Niera for a long time. Sure, she's an egotistical narcissist, but I don't believe she's capable of destroying billions of lives. For what? She already has nearly unlimited power.*

"We need to focus," Megan says. "How much time do we have to formulate a plan to stop it?"

Matt says, "I'm not sure when the invitations will be released. It's a derivative of a multifactor game scenario. Once released, the program says it will take forty-eight hours to aggregate enough hosts to initiate the Farm."

"I can help uncover the timelines," Megan says, her code-breaking instincts tingling. "We have similar logic at Daedalus for managing countless contingencies in space exploration. Let me try to pull this one apart."

While Megan is working on the invitation timing, Matt explores the earliest written code for the Path Program, looking for clues as to who built it.

He motions to Alyssa. "Hey, I found a 'junk' line of code with a numerical key to unlock it. Only, the numbers are not complete." *This is weird. The numbers already filled in are the eight-digit birthdate of my mother followed by an* M, *the eight-digit birthdate of my father followed by an* F, *and my eight-digit birthdate followed by a blank line. Why would the programmer use this sequence and then leave it unfinished for years? What does it open?*

Matt asks Alyssa, "What do you make of this?"

"I don't know, looks like a series of random numbers and letters."

"It's statistically improbable to be random."

"Why?" Alyssa asks.

"Because these numbers represent my mother's, my father's, and my numeric birthdays in order. Twenty-four numbers in a pattern unique to my family is not a coincidence!"

"Why is the last one missing a letter?"

"Exactly." Matt smiles at Alyssa. "It's logical the *M* stands for 'mother' and the *F* for 'father.' What do you think I am?"

"Try *R* for 'robot'?" Alyssa jokes.

Matt sneers. "Since I'm their child, I'll try C." Matt adds the letter, and the line doesn't change.

"One more, I'll try M for 'Matt.'" Again, the line doesn't change.

Alyssa throws out an idea. "You're also their son, so try S."

Matt keys it in and hits enter. The screen flashes a warning, followed by a message: "It's not what you've been told, Matt. I'm in the cube. Find Drazen and stop..." The message ends.

Matt and Alyssa freeze, the shock of the message locking them in place.

"What do you think it means?" Alyssa asks.

"It must be from my father," Matt says, stunned.

"But hasn't he been gone for twenty years?"

"Yes, but this line of code has been sitting idle, just waiting to be discovered and solved. And it's meant for me."

Across the room, Megan screams with delight, disrupting Matt and Alyssa's investigations. "I cracked the instructions on the invitation. It goes live through the AIP at 12:01 a.m. on June thirteenth. That means whoever created it expects to aggregate enough hosts to initiate the Farm by the early-morning hours on June fifteenth."

Alyssa looks at Matt. "That's roughly the same time the second wave is expected to reach Earth."

Megan gasps. "There's another piece of disturbing news. The instructions make reference to a new governing class with a lifespan of hundreds of years."

Before they can process the information, emergency alarms start to sound.

# 34

## THE SECURITY BREACH

Alarms scream throughout the Daedalus buildings.

Alyssa asks Megan, "Is this a test?"

"It's been going on too long, and it's different from our regular compliance sirens," Megan replies. "No, this is something serious."

Megan calls the main entrance.

A panicked voice comes back over the speaker: "We're not equipped to manage a crisis like this. There are too many of them and they're well-armed."

"Who is well-armed, and what did you do?" Megan asks.

"Are you kidding, Megan? We let them through. They promised that everyone would be safe if they were permitted to depart with both packages. I'm sorry, I had no choice. If we resisted, we would have been slaughtered."

"Where are they now?" Megan asks.

"All I know is that they fanned out. I'm guessing they are executing a systematic sweep of each building, starting with the outer perimeter."

Megan turns to Matt and Alyssa, her voice sputtering as she says the obvious. "The two of you are the packages, and you're in a lot of danger. We need to get you out of here, and fast."

Megan says, "We have the advantage right now. We know where they started and I can tap into the video records to see how they progress through the buildings. It will be thirty minutes before they get this deep into the complex."

"That's great, but we don't have any way to protect ourselves, and since they know we're here, we can't simply hide and hope they go away," Alyssa says.

"I agree, but there is a way out. Gaio and I prepared for a scenario like this. Follow close to me, it's going to be a tight squeeze and a steady climb."

"Are you telling me we're going up…where the mercenaries are now searching?" Matt asks.

"Yes, but we're moving away from them. You have to trust me. If we hurry, we will get there first. Now, let's go," Megan demands.

The three move quickly through steep, narrow corridors with alarms ringing overhead.

Megan says, "Here we go. This ladder leads to a secure door that can only be opened from this direction. On the other side is a platform with one of our prototype aerial vehicles. You both can fly out without detection."

Matt says, "Neither of us knows how to fly."

"Thankfully, the drone does," Megan replies. She cracks the door an inch, looks across the platform, and breathes a sigh of relief. "Perfect, it's empty, for now."

Matt and Alyssa step into their seats on the drone. Alyssa asks Megan, "Aren't you coming?"

"No. I'm going to stay and find out as much as I can about who sent them. If the two of you are not here, they'll have no reason to hurt us. We also notified the authorities and expect them to arrive shortly."

Matt and Alyssa debate where they should go, when Megan interrupts, shouting a command into the drone's navigation system. "Location university home." Megan says, "From there, you can get to Gaio."

Matt says, "No offense, but why are we going to him? How can he help us now?"

"More than you believe," Megan answers.

"Okay, but he left without saying where he was going. Where do we find him?" Alyssa asks.

Megan sees a small group of mercenaries in the corridor behind them, moments away. "He's at the Garden, but Gaio never told me its location. He always said, 'If I inform you, you could be forced to disclose it.'"

"That doesn't help us. So, who would know where to find him?" Alyssa asks.

"Find Jenna Zane. She and Gaio go way back, and she will know."

Alyssa and Matt look at each other, confused.

The first mercenary moves down the platform. It's clear there isn't time for any more questions. Megan closes the door, slaps the side of the drone, and raises her hands high into the air, screaming, "Go."

The aircraft accelerates into the desert sky. Jenna Zane's address flashing on the screen.

• • •

Moments later, Megan is surrounded. One of the mercenaries leans in to question her. It's really Fitz asking the questions, remotely controlling the mercenary's body and mind as his proxy. "Where did you send our prize packages?" he asks.

Megan replies, "I helped them escape but have no idea where they're going."

"You're a liar, and a bad one at that. I know you sent them in a pilotless drone. You must have programmed its destination." Fitz instructs the mercenaries to take her inside, away from her colleagues.

In Fitz's bunker hundreds of miles away, Megan's defiance has Fitz's anger growing into a tempest. She has resisted giving any information to endanger Matt and Alyssa, despite a full helping of verbal abuse and minor physical pressure.

Unknown to her, each passing minute also results in another ounce of Fitz's favorite spirit being consumed. The combination of wasting time and getting drunk has hammered his patience.

Fitz scowls and leans into the display. "You do understand I control this man's mind and actions. If I command him to kill you, there would be no hesitation."

"Don't make a mistake. You need me," Megan replies. However, as the interrogation continues, she begins to accept major physical harm as a real possibility.

Her heart thumps louder as she responds to Fitz's latest question. "I can't tell you something I don't know, and I don't have authority to access the vehicle's control systems."

Fitz's voice is cold. "I have given you enough chances. If you won't tell me willingly, I'll take it from you."

Fitz directs the mercenary to apply the mind collar using any force that is needed.

Megan tries to connect directly with the mercenary. "Don't do this. You're making a mistake not of your own free will. Please resist..." Before she can finish her pleading, the device is secure around her neck. Moments later, she's docile, eyes glazed over, locked out of her own head.

Fitz confidently states, "Now, let's try this again."

# 35

## THE JUMP

The prototype drone flies through smooth skies as the sun settles over the western desert landscape. On opposite sides of the aisle, Matt and Alyssa are taking advantage of the luxury leather recliners and have been sleeping the first two hours of their flight.

Alyssa hears a ding and looks up to see an illuminated menu with scores of food and drink options. *If I order something, I'll need to move from my cozy position and get it from the back.* "I remember when flying came with a flight attendant," she says.

"And a pilot." Matt says, having also been woken by the ding. "We should be at the midpoint of our ride. I'm hungry, and the club sandwich sounds perfect right now. Want anything? I'll get it."

"I'll take whatever you're having. Hey, do you think this drone has the proper clearances to land, and what about a flight plan? Doesn't every flight need an approval?"

"We got through the first two hours with no issues, so it's reasonable to assume we're good. Besides, I suspect Megan picked our destination long before trouble arrived."

As they finish their meal, Alyssa asks, "Were you aware Gaio and Jenna knew each other?"

"No, and I should be asking you that question. You knew her a lot better than me, and wasn't his past life part of your pillow talk?"

Just then, the vehicle banks tightly to the right. "That didn't feel normal," Alyssa comments.

Matt says, "I'm not sure what's happening, but there's no chance we're at our destination yet."

Alyssa looks out the window. "We're turning around, and considering we've been in the air less than two and a half hours, we must be somewhere over Arizona."

"Yes, I agree. It's Fitz. He must have gained control of the drone."

"At least Megan couldn't give him Gaio's location."

"Yes, but he will know we were headed to see Jenna," Matt adds, concerned.

Fitz's voice comes over the communication system. "Good evening and welcome to Traitor Airlines. I told you before that you could not escape. I have control of the drone, and I'm bringing you back to the lab. You both have a lot of explaining to do."

Matt pulls Alyssa close. "We can't go back. If we do, they will get what they need and then kill us both."

"Agreed. We need to find a way off this drone!"

"Oh right, like we're going to jump," he says, laughing.

"A mandatory safety rule for drones is to have parachutes available for passengers and an emergency exit door in the back. It's designed to make people feel safer with unmanned flights, even though they have a perfect safety record."

"How do you know that?" Matt asks.

"Learned it joining the mile-high club on one of Gaio's private drones."

"Gross," Matt responds. "Are you recommending we put on a parachute and eject from the drone, at fifteen thousand feet?"

"I know it sounds crazy, but it's our only chance to get away from Fitz. I've done dozens of jumps. We will freefall for about a minute, and then the parachute will automatically engage and guide us down. We don't need to worry about commercial aircraft, as they fly much higher than drones."

Matt feels dizzy. "You will be okay, but I've never done this before."

Alyssa smiles, pulls Matt close, and in a calm voice says, "Then it's my turn to save you."

She double-checks the tandem parachute. "We'll only have fifteen seconds after opening this door before it automatically closes again."

Grabbing Matt's hand tightly, she says, "I'll get you to the ground safely, but the first step is a long one. Keep your legs back and your arms spread wide."

She opens the back door and kisses his cheek before they jump out the back of the drone.

As they descend toward Earth, the cold high-altitude air changes to a warm Arizona breeze, escorting them through the evening sky. The light from a full moon makes it easy to navigate over the hills and valleys.

Alyssa pulls the guide ropes and says, "Once we get a little lower, we should look for the best place to land. I'll have control over a two-square-mile radius."

Matt points to the lights of a small, remote town flickering below. "Not sure if it's deserted, but land over there. I have a plan."

The pair makes a smooth touchdown a quarter mile from the outskirts of town.

Matt says, "Perfect, I don't think anyone saw us. Let's go over and see what we can find."

# 36

## THE UPDATE

The bright moon's position behind the GOD headquarters casts a dark shadow over the courtyard used as the company's helipad. Fitz's men are strategically positioned, awaiting the arrival of the packages.

Fitz stands in the middle giving verbal commands as the whirling sounds from the drone's vertical-descent blades cut out, causing Fitz to smile like a child at Christmas. Tossing his computer to the ground, he unholsters his weapon and approaches the drone's passenger stairs.

"Hey, Chief, do you want me to check it out first?" Lieutenant Brass asks.

"Not a chance. I've waited a long time for this moment. I'm not letting anyone else have the satisfaction of seeing the fear in their faces." He leaps the four steps, unable to control his excitement, like a kid waiting to unwrap his presents, and steps into the cabin.

The only sounds heard after are plates crashing to the

ground. Fitz comes out, lightning in his eyes, cursing into the sky.

"So, what's next, Chief?" Brass asks.

Fitz remains still for a moment, looking puzzled. "You know what's next. We go after the bastards, and when we find them, there will be no more negotiating. Get your team ready to leave. But first, I need to have a talk with the big boss."

Niera's assistant, Jacob, looks up to see Fitz exiting the elevator and moves in front of Niera's office door. "You will have to come back later. You don't have an appointment, and Niera doesn't want to be disturbed," Jacob says.

Fitz scowls and accelerates his pace. In a booming voice, he warns Jacob, "If you do not move by the time I get to the door, I'm going to hit you so hard even this company's advanced technology won't be able to put you back together again." *I really hope he holds his position. I need to hit someone.*

Jacob feigns a call coming in and hurries back to his desk.

Fitz bursts through the door to find Drazen standing unusually close to Niera. Caught by surprise, Drazen jerks away while cursing at Fitz. "Don't you know to knock before coming in here?"

Fitz disregards Drazen's question and focuses his gaze on Niera. *She looks strange. Almost as if she is in a trance.* He asks, "Niera, are you okay?"

"I'm fine. How are you?" she replies in a robotic tone. "How is your pursuit of Boson and Starr going?"

*She's really acting weird.* "Not good. I thought we had them trapped in a damn drone, but don't worry, I will get those bastards!"

"Well, I'm sure you have a plan to remedy the situation."

*That's the extent of her anger? Normally she would rip me a new one.* "Ma'am, I thought you would be more impassioned about their escape," Fitz says as he tries to get closer to Niera.

Drazen pulls him away, making an excuse for her. "She's got a lot on her mind right now. It's best if we continue our conversation outside and let Niera focus on her day job."

Fitz notices Jacob has left the floor. *Too easy. I'd be proud of myself if he weren't such a coward to start with.*

The two men talk a few minutes before Fitz pushes the down elevator button.

"Find them, Fitz!" Drazen demands.

"I will. Just as soon as they pop back up on the grid."

"Why is that important? He's at a level requiring a locator implant. Use it."

"Boson has gone dark, very smart of him to remove it."

"Surely a resourceful person such as yourself could guess what their next steps would be." Drazen's statement reeks of sarcasm, as he hopes to elicit a response from Fitz.

"I can, damn it, but it will require a hybrid approach, something more low-tech. They're smart enough to avoid locations that could trigger a sighting, which means they will primarily be in the backcountry."

"Just take care of it," Drazen says as he walks away.

*Goodbye to you too. No time to waste.* Fitz calls Lieutenant Brass and gives him orders to assemble a team of ex-soldiers, mercenaries, ATVs, bloodhounds, and anything else he needs to hunt them down. He adds, "Search all the small towns and back roads between their last known location and the address I'm sending you now."

Before hanging up, Fitz offers a fortune of platform credits to the person who brings them in.

Fitz glances back at the closed office door. *Do I go back and see what's up? She didn't look right.* He moves toward the office but is stopped by an incoming call.

"What the hell, Brass," Fitz says. Moments later, Fitz responds, "I'll be right there." *She's a big girl. She can take care of herself.*

The elevator door opens, and Jacob peers around the corner, knees shaking.

"Don't worry, I have bigger fish to catch." Fitz chuckles as he hears Jacob breathe a ponderous sigh of relief.

Niera is alone in her office, having stood in the same spot for the past several minutes. A faint knock gets her attention. She moves toward the bathroom and looks into the mirror, observing her own unusual behavior.

She's fighting an internal battle, her mind flashing between different images of windows, then a skyscraper, and lastly a forest. Moving inches from the mirror, she sees her face and then a man's face. "John Boson," she screams.

# 37

## THE MECHANIC

Alyssa and Matt make the short trek through the desert and see a tilted sign hanging on by the last of its eight rusty bolts. "Welcome to Hot Springs" is barely visible after years of baking in the hot sun.

Alyssa comments, "There's an eerie darkness at the edge of this town," as chills run up her spine.

"It looks like the people either have moved or are holed up in their houses, most likely glued to the AIP, as all other activities in the town have long gone."

"The service station is lit up. Perhaps it's open," Alyssa says.

"Open or not, look under the carport. There's a vintage Ford F-150. It looks to be in excellent condition despite its age, and we need it."

"Why that truck?"

Matt replies, "It's dependable, but more importantly, it doesn't need connected technology to run."

"Okay, but we can't steal it," insists Alyssa.

"I know, let's go to the main building and see if anyone is home. Maybe we can make a trade for it."

Alyssa gives him a strange look. "A trade? All we have are the clothes on our backs, and I'm not sure yours would get us a toy truck."

"Exactly, but yours might." He smirks.

"What do you have in mind?" she asks suspiciously.

Matt avoids the question and steps onto the porch. The first board creaks, but on his second step, he snaps one of the thin pieces of wood. "Oh, crap, that's going to wake someone up."

"I don't think so," Alyssa says while looking through a dirty front window. "There's an old man slumped over the desk wearing nothing but a mechanic's shirt and his ARC. He's hopelessly lost in the platform," she says sadly.

"This will be easier than I thought," Matt mumbles. "Let's go in and look for the F-150's keys."

They move around the office. "Do you see anything?" he asks.

"Nothing."

"I'm going to unplug him," Matt says.

"Be careful. You know what they say about waking a sleepwalker."

Matt pulls the power connector out of the computer. The mechanic stiffens, frantically waving his hand, trying to grasp the cord and reconnect it.

Matt coughs.

"What the hell are you doing?" the mechanic yells. "I was just about to make it with my girlfriend."

*A case of coitus interruptus, yuck!* Alyssa looks at Matt, who is nodding his head toward the mechanic.

She shakes her head and shoots visual daggers back at him. *Oh no, he can't be thinking that.*

The mechanic tries to stand, then remembers he's only wearing a shirt. He quickly drops back into his chair.

"We want to buy your F-150, or at least rent it for a few days," Matt says. "It doesn't look like you get out much anyway."

"Get out of here. She's in perfect condition and not for sale or rent," the mechanic says defiantly.

Wide-eyed, Matt looks at Alyssa again, encouraging her to engage.

*He's going to pay for this later.* Alyssa gags but nods her understanding.

She unbuttons one more button of her blouse, moves in front of the desk, leans over, and places her hands next to the mechanic's. "You must be really good with your hands to keep your truck in such good shape."

A half smile forms on the mechanic's face.

*Got him,* she thinks to herself with confidence. "How about you come outside and start her up. Let me look under the hood."

The mechanic breaks out in laughter. "Please, don't you think I know what you're doing? No city girl in a thousand-dollar outfit is going to come out here and be interested in anything I do. Besides, my girlfriend Bunny is wayyyy hotter than you."

"And she's probably a four-hundred-pound guy named Frank," Alyssa exclaims.

Turning to Matt, she says, "It's your turn now." *This ought to be worth the price of admission.* She finds a little humor in the irony of the situation. *All I need now is a little popcorn.*

Matt paces the floor and then says, "Instead of money, what if I offer you a more valuable currency?"

"Like what? I already told her I have a hot girlfriend."

"Platform credits."

The mechanic stands up.

*Oh, God, please sit down. I think I'm going to be sick.* Alyssa turns and looks out the same window she peered into a few minutes ago.

"How many, and can I use them for the dark corners of the platform?"

Matt replies, "One thousand, and yes, if it's your thing."

*Of course it's his thing. Can't you see his "thing" right now?*

Matt extends his hand to finalize the agreement but retracts it at the last moment. "No need to shake, I trust you."

*Smart move.*

"I'll need your computer to get into my account," Matt says.

"No funny business," warns the mechanic.

Moments later, the credits arrive, and he hands Matt the keys. "Take what you want. I'm going to be busy for quite a while with my girlfriends. And after that, I can explore the Path Program."

They stop dead in their tracks and turn back to the mechanic.

Alyssa comments, "I heard what he said, but it's too late. He's reengaged, lost to his fantasies."

Matt says, "I had to access my company account to get the credits. I suspect they're monitoring my activity and will be onto us soon. We need to get going."

They fill the F-150 and two extra ten-gallon cans with gas and grab food supplies and a tablet from the office.

The engine purrs as they head out.

"We need to keep off the major highways," Alyssa says.

A dust cloud rises from the desert floor as they drive into the night.

# 38

## THE NIGHT SKY

The F-150 comes to a fork in the road outside of Beatty, Nevada.

Matt says, "It's a good idea for us to eat something and get some sleep before the sun comes up. We can't risk parking on the shoulder, so we need to find someplace with more cover."

Matt pulls off the narrow two-lane road, driving slowly over the loose gravel, navigating between the rolling hills until the truck is not visible from the road. He puts the truck in park and turns the engine off. "Feels good to drive again. For the past several years, I've been mostly in the back of autonomous vehicles."

The truck sits tucked behind a small hill, hidden from the rare early morning passerby. They roll up the windows, and Matt turns off the headlights. The air is calm, so they wait a few minutes before getting out, allowing the dust kicked up from their tires to dissipate.

Minutes later, Alyssa lies in the cargo bed looking at

the stars. "The air smells clean, and the light from the full moon is deceiving," she says. "I was always fascinated with the stars as a little girl." She points up, making a full 360-degree sweep of the sky, calling out star clusters, nebula, visible corporate satellites, and space stations.

Matt listens as if he were a student in one of Alyssa's classes. "They look like a symphony of nature and technology mixed together and thrown onto the canvas of our universe," he adds.

"What a deep observation, Mr. Boson."

"What, don't you believe I'm capable of appreciating the office in which you work and live?"

Alyssa smiles, makes a few other celestial observations, and props herself up on her elbow. Moving closer to Matt, she asks, "Why have you never married? And don't say because of me."

"It's simple logic. Numbers and code are easy. People are harder, too many variables, known and unknown. You can build an entire system of analytics, of hard math, with unknowns and even irrationalities accounted for. But people operate on their own internal math filled with emotions, like a program of contradicting irrationalities."

"How so, Mr. Spock?" she asks, pleasantly amused.

"What I say to someone might have a completely different impact depending on whether they had lunch or sex recently. And then I think about all the unknowns, variables, compounded and extrapolated as they interact with each other and their precipitant outcomes, the offshoots, the fractal multiverse of possibilities...until every approach to an interaction becomes laden with its own impossibly dense weight...its own gravity. There's no predictability for an outcome regardless of how well I have studied the materials. No, thank you. Numbers are much easier than people. And they don't disappear on you."

Alyssa looks at him with a mix of awe, bewilderment, and finally, pity. "So, there's never been anyone?"

Matt looks away. *Only one.* "Perhaps if I had done some 'enhancements' a long time ago, it would have helped me compete, to find someone interested in me."

Alyssa grabs Matt's hand. "Don't ever say anything like that again. You're real, and your inner strength is more than enough to compete with anyone."

"Anyone?" he fires back.

She lies back down and sees a pair of meteors streak across the sky. Alyssa points to them and asks, "What do you think it's a sign of?"

"Not sure." *I think it's the universe's way of acknowledging you're the closest I ever came to finding love.* "We should turn in. We'll need to start again in a couple of hours if we want to stay ahead of Fitz."

Alyssa places her head on his chest and closes her eyes. She listens to his rapid heartbeat affirm what she's feeling. She kisses him and says, "Yes, anyone," and for the next hour, sleep is the last thing on their minds.

At the same time in Hot Springs, Arizona, Fitz and a small team burst into the lobby of the mechanic's shop. Fitz stares at the man and then addresses Lieutenant Brass. "Can you believe this guy is so immersed in the platform he didn't hear us break through his fucking door?"

"You want me to get his ass up?" Brass asks with the devotion of a dog.

"Don't get anywhere near him," Fitz barks back. "Look at what he's doing...disgusting."

"If we don't disengage him, how will we get the information we need?"

"It's rather simple," Fitz says. "We know who he is and what he's doing. It will be easy to motivate him to tell us what we want. Hand me your computer. I have a surprise for him."

Fitz logs into the AIP and uses a voluptuous avatar to interact with the mechanic. A short while later, her digital booty call from the dark corner of the platform persuades the mechanic to disclose information on Matt and Alyssa.

"Deplorables are so easy to manipulate," Fitz says. "Soon, the world will be rid of them and better off for it." Fitz communicates the direction they were traveling and the license plate number to his remote mercenaries and says, "Find them at all costs, but I want them alive!"

# 39

## THE CONNECTOR

A streak of sunlight rises over the hill and warms the otherwise-cool morning air. Matt and Alyssa lie comfortably under tarps in the cargo bed of the truck, still locked in the embrace that made sleep possible hours ago. The early-morning air carries the subtle scent from the numerous barrel cactus clinging to life on the harsh desert hillside.

Matt covers his eyes and tries to get a few more minutes of sleep. "No use." He sits up. "We need to meet with Jenna."

His motion and voice wake up Alyssa, who says, "Well good morning to you too."

"I'm sorry. Good morning."

"It was nice again last night...becoming a regular thing with us," Alyssa says, sitting up, hoping for a reply.

"Yes, very nice. I wish we weren't under these conditions though...but nice no matter where we are."

*That may be the best I can get from him. I'll need to*

*soften him up when the time is right. Now, we need to focus on our immediate needs.* With Matt looking off into the distance, she says, "I agree about Jenna, but how do we risk getting close to her? She works and lives in a surveilled environment."

"You're right. We need to assume our enemies will be waiting for us there. We can use a proxy; someone inside GOD we can get to visit her."

Puzzled, Alyssa asks, "How are you going to do that?"

"I'll need a universal access device for the laptop we took from the mechanic. Unfortunately, we have to risk a trip into Beatty...to visit a computer repair store."

"Won't that put us in too much danger of being seen?" Alyssa asks.

"I think it's a risk we must take, and besides, with the remoteness of the area, we have limited exposure to surveillance cameras." They jump into the truck, moments later pulling onto the road for the short drive to the city's outskirts.

Alyssa stares out the window at the varying shades of brown and orange the desert presents. *No trees, hardly any shrubbery, and yet its consistency over time is beautiful. The sand, pebbles, and boulders don't care about the advancing technologies. They can't be controlled, and they will be here long after we're all gone. I've never felt so conscious and concerned about things like cameras. In fact, I hardly ever noticed they were there. Now, as we run for our lives, clinging to the safety of the remote wilderness, I'm painfully aware of them and the life-and-death consequences of being captured by their glass lenses.*

Alyssa calls out, "Look over there. Turn right now!"

Without hesitation, Matt slams on the brakes and veers into the parking lot. A black skid mark and cloud of gray dust are evidence of how dangerous the turn was. The truck faces a run-down building with a green illuminated welcome sign.

Matt comments, "He may have been a perv, but he has kept the brakes in good shape."

Alyssa flashes a sign of disgust and says, "If they're open, we may be safe. Given the looks of the place, I doubt they're on the grid."

The front door swings open, crashing into the wall behind it. The door handle fits perfectly into a hole in the drywall from dozens of previous openings.

A woman peers over the counter and asks, "What can I do you for?"

Matt steps over piles of broken equipment and furniture to hand her the tablet. "I need a way to connect this to the rest of the world."

She chuckles. "You're kidding, right? This tablet is old enough to earn a spot in my antique display over there." She points to where Alyssa is standing.

Alyssa looks in the case. *What's a BlackBerry?*

The clerk studies the couple. "You don't look like the kind of people who rely on old equipment. You both have a peculiar 'aura' of privilege about you. If you give me your GOD identification number, I'll upload the laptop with new software, your preferences, and data."

Matt cuts her off. "We don't have one."

"You don't...you don't have one?"

"Nope."

She grabs her chin. "You some kind of time traveler or from the government?"

*This is going sideways. She's suspicious of Matt.* Watching her feet to keep from tripping over the wires crisscrossing the floor, Alyssa weaves around the display cases to stand in front of the counter.

"Excuse me, ma'am, my friend and I may seem odd to you, but we have honest intentions. Looking at the condition of this place and knowing you choose to keep your shop far from the influence of GOD, I hope you can trust we're not much different from you other than our ages. We like our privacy but need some information, which is why we need the connector, and just the connector."

Moments later, Alyssa walks out of the shop grinning ear to ear while holding what they came for. She turns her head to hide how pleased she is and pats Matt on the back. "You see, sometimes your handsome demeanor is not enough to get the ladies to do what you want."

Matt stops at the driver's-side door, looks into the F-150's side-view mirror, and smiles. "Oh, but it's enough to get you to do what I want."

Alyssa peers through the cab of the truck and gives Matt a mean, playful look. *Not always, or have you forgotten?*

The doors close, and Matt reaches for her hand. "Thank you for stepping in. I know I was sinking fast."

After filling the truck with gas, they return to the spot from last night. Matt says, "This location was lucky for me once. Let's try it again."

Alyssa's eyebrows rise up. "You're not implying we jump back into the cab, are you?"

"Well, under any other circumstance, the answer is yes. Right now, however, we need to find Jenna."

"How exactly are you going to pull that off from here?" She looks baffled.

"Every GOD employee has some type of implant, and each one has a backdoor entry via a visual binary code, allowing access to the system's BIOS. It's designed to provide a minimally invasive approach for diagnostics, resets, and troubleshooting. They're rarely used, which is why employees allow them to do it."

"Are the implants like the one we cut out of you at Daedalus?"

"No. It's counterintuitive, but my implant was less sophisticated. It served the single purpose of location tracking for executives. Lower-level employees have other safety functions, including hijacking their communication and neuro systems. If I can get someone to scan their retina, I can install a slave malware program called Geppetto and take control of them."

"That doesn't sound legal, or like anything most people would willingly agree to."

"Truthfully, the control part was never disclosed to employees."

"Your employer is looking better to me each day...how unethical."

"No time to debate that point. What I need is for my target to open an attachment."

Alyssa says, "How do you know about the Geppetto program?"

"It's my job. I have to make sure our systems aren't vulnerable to similar attacks. I often browse the dark web, observing and monitoring all nefarious activity, and Fitz sends me new malware to ensure our systems are protected against emerging viruses."

"But you're engineers. Who among you would be dumb enough to open an unsolicited attachment?"

Matt responds immediately. "I've got some ideas."

# 40

## THE PROXIES

At the GOD quantum lab, a lecherous employee, Cory, makes his way down the hall, checking out one of the female employees overtly and gratuitously. She catches him and he looks away awkwardly.

Matt adds Cory's name into the recipient line. He moves to the subject line and hovers for a minute. "No point in being coy," he says and adds, "Click Here for Backdoor Entry."

Cory returns to his desk, cluttered with pinups, and sees a new email pop up. He looks around to see if the coast is clear, moves close to the screen, and opens the attachment. His screen flashes once, followed by a series of successive, intervallic flashes, all of which hit the man like a blast of stifling air.

• • •

The tablet rests on the dashboard of the F-150. Matt and Alyssa keep an eye on the screen as the circle spins. Alyssa shuffles side to side. "These old trucks are not very comfortable. The front seats barely recline."

Matt is about to respond when a visual from the Geppetto program appears, showing a marionette controlled by a puppeteer. "We have him. Now let's take him for a little stroll. Everything he sees will appear on our screen, and I can control his language."

"This is weird stuff," Alyssa says.

Cory stands, clumsily making his way out of the lab, his eyes focused on the exit door.

A female coworker notices his glazed eyes and awkward movements, and asks, "Are you okay?"

There's no reply as the door closes behind him.

She shakes her head, happy to be rid of him.

Jenna is home having lunch when she hears a chaotic knocking at the front door. Peering through the peephole, she sees a man she doesn't recognize. She latches the chain lock before turning the handle, partially opening the door. "What do you want?" she asks.

"Please open the door so we can talk," Cory says, standing inches from the opening.

Jenna shuts the door, yelling, "Go away!"

Cory responds, "Please wait, Jenna. This is Matt Boson. I'm using this person as a proxy. It was too dangerous for me to come to you in person."

Jenna presses her back to the door and sits down. "I don't believe it's you, Matt. This person could just as easily be one of Fitz's henchmen."

"I understand your concern, but I can prove who I am." Matt relays the information about his father that she shared with him a few days ago. "You told me you haven't shared this information with anyone, so you must believe it's me."

She stands, knowing it's him. The door opens, and she says, "This is some dark tech you're meddling with, kiddo."

"These are desperate times, but before we get into that, you should know Alyssa is sitting beside me. We've been on quite an adventure together these past days."

Matt provides Jenna with a play-by-play of events culminating with their narrow escape from the Daedalus compound.

"I knew you would be able to help each other, perhaps even..."

Alyssa cuts in. "No need to go down that path. The subject at hand is finding Gaio, and his colleague Megan said you would know where we can find him. Is that true?"

Jenna takes a deep breath and begins. "Matt, there's more to the story than I shared days ago."

"Oh great. I haven't even had time to process what you've already told me."

Alyssa takes hold of Matt's hand. "Don't worry, I'm here with you now. We can handle anything, as long as it's the truth."

Matt smiles.

Jenna continues. "I didn't know Gaio well, but I met

him a long time ago when I was working with Niera on advanced medical treatments."

Matt shakes his head. "Wait, you worked with Gaio and Niera?"

"Before you react negatively, let me finish filling in the pieces. We met at the lab where work was advancing on synthetic stem cell technology. We were able to embed quantum nanocomputers within synthetic stem cells. The result was revolutionary. When we injected the synthetic stem cells, they attached to every unique cell type, learning its function. When the original cell died, the synthetic cell replaced it. A person injected with enough synthetic cells should live several hundred years."

"What role did Gaio play in all of this?"

"Gaio participated in a consultant capacity only. I started to sense a building conflict he had with Niera and a more overt one with Drazen. The tech development went very well. Then something serious happened, causing Gaio to have a falling-out."

"What falling-out?" Matt snaps back.

"When you find him, he can tell you. I was just an observer."

Alyssa says, "I'll ask again, where can we find him?"

Jenna says, "Matt, do you remember the secret cabin your father built and the land he bought, the one you used to go fishing at?"

He says, "Yes, but how do you..."

Jenna interrupts. "Never mind that for now, and don't say its location aloud. After everything you told me, I'm worried about my residence, and even my office, being under surveillance."

Matt asks, "What relevance could my father's old property have to us today? It was sold when he disappeared."

Jenna says, "The land was sold to Gaio, who has since developed it into a compound equipped with various resources you can use. Are you sure you know where it is?"

He says, "I was young, and the memories have faded, but I can get close enough to sniff it out."

Jenna receives a call from her neighbor, asking, "Why are all those cars lined up..."

Just then, Jenna's front door is kicked in. A dozen of Fitz's men storm through, placing a mind-control collar on Cory and then surrounding Jenna.

"Who the hell are you, and what gives you the right to smash into my home?" she screams.

One of the men steps in front of Jenna, eyes glazed over. "It's me, Fitz. I'm sorry I'm not there in person." Fitz's proxy looks over at Cory. "I can see you're familiar with how this works. Now let me see who is in control of him."

Fitz's proxy examines the code from Cory's implant. "Geppetto...hmm."

It looks into Cory's eyes, using them as a direct camera to Matt. "Looks like you've improved it since I gave it to you, Matt. You were always my best beta tester."

It then moves over to Jenna. "In the spirit of truth, allow me to dispel a few more subterfuges."

Cory says, "Leave her alone. She hasn't done anything. She's innocent."

Fitz's proxy smirks and says, "I wouldn't go that far,"

as he commands the other soldiers to hold Jenna down. The proxy places his hands over Jenna's face, rubbing his thumbs over her eyes. He pushes in and twists.

Through Cory, Matt pleads, "Stop! Stop!"

Fitz's proxy turns around smiling and holds his hands up. "Relax, she's fine. I was just helping her with her lenses." The proxy has two brown contact lenses in his hands. He then steps away to show Jenna's face, now with shimmering blue eyes.

Matt and Alyssa watch from the tablet screen, baffled. "What did you do to her?"

The proxy replies, "When Jenna said she was involved early, but left on principle, she undersold her level of involvement."

Jenna looks at Cory, her face a mask of concession and apology. "I'm a woman of science, of education, of learning. Consider the possibilities if we possess unlimited time. Imagine what we would learn and teach. Yes, I did inject myself with synthetic quantum stem cells, but I also left on principle when Niera and her handlers refused to share the innovation beyond their own pack."

"Enough guilt cleansing," Fitz's proxy says. "You did not play by the rules you agreed to. For some reason, you had to get back in his life, bringing this down on you both. Well, the Lord giveth, and I taketh away." Fitz initiates a senescence protocol, deactivating Jenna's synthetic stem cells.

Jenna suddenly begins convulsing, falling to the ground moments later. She struggles to find enough strength to lift her head from the floor and looks directly at Cory, pleading, "I'm sorry, I never finished telling you..."

Her face suddenly looks thirty years older, flesh pulled taut over her cheekbones, her black hair turned gray. She stops talking and, moments later, lies in a lifeless heap on the floor.

The silence in the room is broken as Fitz's proxy turns to Cory, leans in, and says, "I warned you those you loved would suffer. If you agree to come in now, of your own accord, there's no need for further casualties. If I must work to find you, there will be more death, and it will be on your hands."

As Cory's head slumps forward, Matt's program is terminated.

One of Fitz's henchmen asks, "What should we do, kill him?"

"No, bring him back to the office. We'll pull the data and see what he heard and saw. Once we have what we need, we wipe him clean and send him on his way. He won't remember anything."

Alyssa's and Matt's vision blurs as waves of memory flash through their minds. A sharp pain knots their stomachs, confirming what they're seeing. Jenna is dead!

Matt pulls the last tissue from the box under the dashboard and hands it to Alyssa. She whispers, "What just happened?"

"We witnessed how desperate someone is to keep us from disclosing the truth, desperate enough to kill Jenna."

"Who can we trust?" Alyssa swallows, struggling to comprehend the truth. "Where could we possibly be safe? And how do we just leave her there on the floor?"

Facts, suspicions, and unanswered questions swirl in Matt's mind like pieces of a jigsaw puzzle. "Whatever we've stumbled into cost Jenna her life. The best way to assure she didn't die in vain is to finish what we started. There are only three days until the opt-in, and two more before the initiation. It sounds cold, but we don't have time to mourn her death."

Alyssa nods. "After what I just witnessed, I can't believe I'm going to say this. Where are we going now?"

"Idaho, and we need to be there in twelve hours."

Fitz pours himself a double and downs it in one swallow. He stares at Jenna's body. "This must be my lucky day. A fire drone camera just picked up the truck's license plates near Death Valley National Park."

Fitz plots a line from the mechanic's shop to the drone sighting. "I have their direction and speed. Your friends should be somewhere in here." He draws a circle on the map.

# 41

## THE TRAP

Drazen finishes a virtual meeting and looks over the railing of his patio, seventy floors up in one of the most prestigious buildings in the city.

His security display flashes, "You have a visitor."

*There's no one I want to see today, and besides, who would have the gall to show up without an invitation on a Saturday?* "Tell them to go away. I'm not having any visitors today," Drazen responds.

The robotic security attendant replies, "Sir, it's a Ms. Kristain, and she says she's coming up even if I try to stop her. Should I call the police?"

*What the fuck does she want? I'm getting so tired of babysitting her. At least it's almost over.* "No, go ahead and let her up."

Drazen unlocks the door and returns to his chair on the patio. *She's the CEO. I'm sure she can figure out how to let herself in. And besides, I'm not a damn footman.*

Niera opens the door. "Drazen?" she calls.

"I'm on the patio. Come in."

Niera steps onto the patio but doesn't sit down.

Drazen stares at her pacing back and forth. *This is very erratic, even for her.* "Calm down and take a seat. Tell me what you're experiencing," he says.

"How can I stay calm? I can't get control of my own thoughts. I need someone to help me, but I'm not sure who I can trust. No one does their job. People are plotting against me. I feel I'm being followed." She looks over the rail and into the sky, asking, "Do you think it's safe being out here...exposed?"

"We're safe, but come inside so you can relax." *This is not good. Did I increase the intensity of the neuro-control program too much? I can't have her go off the deep end...yet. I need her to continue to engage with the AIP to get her final instructions through her avatar.*

Niera asks, "Can I close my eyes a minute?"

"Of course, relax."

Although Drazen is committed to his plan, moments of doubt still creep in, especially when it comes to Niera. Fortunately, he's skilled at talking himself out of such weakness.

Watching her like this gives him both pleasure and sadness. After all, she created the foundation for the mind-controlling neuroreceptors now tormenting her. It's like a cocktail of drugs without the needle. He simply hijacked a piece of her work, and stole a few things from the archives, for "bigger" purposes.

He's convinced she has never considered him her equal. Drazen stares at her and thinks, *Look at her now, a monkey begging for help from a future God.*

Minutes later, Niera says, "I feel better, more like me. What were we talking about?"

*I must give her some credit. Most people would be crushed by what I'm hitting her with. She has a strong will, and it's in direct conflict for superiority with my programming.* "We were talking about Boson and how close he is to finishing his investigation."

"Right. I want to reach out to him myself. I'm tired of waiting for others to convince him to come in. We have a good relationship, and he trusts me."

"That's not the best move. We can't risk having Boson lead his friends, our enemies, right to your doorstep. No, we need Fitz to find him and soften him up first."

Drazen gets a call. "Speak of the devil. I'll be right back."

"Hurry, I feel funny, like I'm losing control again."

"What do you want, Fitz?" demands Drazen.

"I have a good idea where Boson and Starr are going."

"Where is it, and why are you sure?"

"We got a hit from a fire drone camera. They're heading north through Nevada. Considering they're on the run, our artificial intelligence program gives it an eighty-two-percent probability he's going to a place where his knowledge of the local geography and its lack of connectivity give him an advantage. His father had a cabin in a remote area of Idaho."

Drazen's eyes light up. "Did you say Idaho?"

"Yes."

"Perfect, I know someone with an estate there. I'll get back to you with instructions. In the meantime, start closing the circle around him."

Drazen grabs a mind-control collar and returns to Niera. "I talked it over with Fitz and we agree with you. Let's get Boson to visit you at your estate near Boise."

"Why there and not the office?"

Drazen ignores the question, sits next to Niera, and holds her hand. "I'm worried about you, Niera. You're not yourself. I may be the only one who understands you, the only one you can trust. I've been at your side all along."

"I know."

"Let me look at your hardware. I may be able to see something we can fix." Drazen puts the collar on Niera, who goes limp. *A few quick instructions for your talk track with Boson, and then I'll bring you back. Done, now let's wake you up so you can call Boson on the way to your private jet. We need to get there before he does and set the trap.*

Alyssa grabs the tablet from between the seats. "Matt, the tablet is vibrating."

"That's odd. I'll pull over."

"It's an incoming message from Niera Kristain. Why would she be trying to contact you now?"

"No idea. A better question is how she knew about this tablet."

"I have a bad feeling about this. Our plan is to find Gaio and use his resources to help us blow the lid off the whole thing," Alyssa says with concern.

"I'd say the same thing if I were you. I just don't believe Niera is behind it all. I've known her for too long. She has issues but has genuinely worked to find solutions for the masses, not destroy them."

Alyssa says, "I'm not as sure as you are. How could so many GOD resources be after us if she's not involved?"

"Not sure." Matt activates the tablet's audio function. "I'm going to respond."

"I don't agree," Alyssa says one final time.

"Good morning, Niera. Why are you calling me?" Matt asks.

Niera's usual aggressive tone is gone. Quietly, she says, "Thank you for picking up. I've been hearing some unsettling things about you and someone named Alyssa Starr. I find them hard to believe, and I'd like to hear your side of the story."

"My side of the story is that you or someone at GOD is trying to kill us."

Suddenly, Niera's demeanor flips. She jumps straight to the issue and asks aggressively, "Are you plotting against me, against the company you work for?"

"You should know I would never do those things," Matt replies.

"Then why did you run?" Niera snaps back.

"I didn't run. I went looking for the answers you put me in charge of finding. I hit a brick wall in the lab, and with Fitz breathing down my neck, I had to find other solutions."

"Okay then, what did you find about our server disruptions?"

"There's a logical explanation for what happened, but there's a much bigger matter to discuss. Someone is using GOD's global infrastructure and influence to execute a plan against the world's population," Matt says.

"That sounds crazy, Matt, but we need to trust each other. Would you be willing to meet me somewhere private, away from any chance of surveillance, to discuss what you have found? I'm at my country house near Boise for a weekend of rest and relaxation. If you come here, we can work it out together. And if you're with Alyssa, she's welcome to come too. I'd love to meet her."

Matt agrees. "Send me the address and I'll be there this evening."

Alyssa's eyes well up. "You know the risk you're taking. A good deal of evidence points to her being behind our pursuit, and you're going to walk right into her home, in the middle of the remote countryside. And isn't it an odd coincidence she's inviting us to her place along the same route we're traveling to find Gaio? Why not simply ask us to come back to the office?"

"When you say it like that...but I have a feeling I should trust her. I can't explain why."

"You never go by feelings when making decisions. You look objectively at the data and pick the most logical solution. Going to her house is not the best decision." After thinking for a minute, she asks, "Are you willing to put your life at risk?"

Matt answers quickly. "Yes."

"Are you willing to put my life at risk?" Alyssa asks, her eyes fixed on him, uncertain of his pending response.

Matt does not hesitate. "Never, which is why it's best for you to continue on, to find Gaio."

"I won't leave you," Alyssa says firmly. "We're safer together. Haven't we already proven we can get out of some sticky situations?"

"We do seem to make a strong team."

They program the directions to Niera's estate and head back onto the road.

# 42

## THE ESTATE

The F-150 approaches the driveway of Niera's grand estate late in the evening. Alyssa's heart pounds, and her mind races with thoughts they may be only minutes away from being captured, tortured, or even worse. Branches from dense rows of tall birch trees lining the driveway make it look more like a forbidding cave than a welcoming passage.

Alyssa comments, "It's odd there's nothing to indicate we're expected. The light posts are all turned off, the guard station is unstaffed, and the security gate is down. I can see a faint glow from front porch lights, but between here and there is complete darkness. If I didn't trust her so much, I'd say the scene is set perfectly for a trap."

Matt replies, "Agree, we need to be on guard," trying to lighten the mood.

She forces a half smile. "Awful pun."

"I know, sorry."

As they reach the parking area near the front doors,

the full magnitude of the house comes into view. The bright moon sits high in the sky behind the estate, casting a dark shadow across the grounds.

Alyssa leans forward for a better look. "There's a waste-disposal tunnel coming out the third-story window. She must be doing some remodeling. Other than that, it seems deserted."

The truck settles into a parking spot. Niera opens the front door and rushes over to give Matt a hug.

She studies Alyssa for a long moment before speaking. "Welcome, and thank you both for coming. I know we have a lot to discuss." She lowers her voice and takes Matt's hand. "Come on, Alyssa. I'd like to show you around."

Alyssa follows, walking with as much confidence as she can muster as Niera leads them from room to room. Niera keeps a good pace but spends little time discussing the house and more on reminiscing with Matt, retelling old stories of teamwork and trust between them.

*This doesn't feel right. She sounds programmed, and why the reminiscing when we're here to discuss a global disaster linked to GOD?* Alyssa asks, "Can we go to the third floor to see what construction you're doing?"

"No, it's not safe for you there." Niera's eyes twitch. She takes a moment to gather herself before continuing. "Let's talk in the library."

They each settle into comfortable chairs by the two-story fireplace.

Niera pours two glasses of a special reserve wine and hands them to her guests.

Alyssa leans toward Matt and says in a hushed tone,

"Everything feels staged. There are no staff, but the wood is freshly stacked, and I have doubts about her starting this fire."

"Yes, it feels a little too safe," he replies.

Niera begins by talking about the company, the escalating pressure due to unsolved system issues, feelings of not being herself, and unseen other forces. She speaks continuously, ignores feedback, and rarely looks at Matt or Alyssa.

Alyssa prods Matt, "This is all interesting, but we need to get what we came for."

"Yes, but she's on a roll, and it would be rude to stop her."

"Not for me." Alyssa interrupts Niera. "There isn't a lot of time to waste. We're here to discuss your system failures and what may be happening in the near future."

Niera's eyes narrow, and her voice sharpens. "Go on then," she says, cutting through the interruption.

Alyssa describes the binary neutron stars, the gravitational waves, and the unlikely coincidence of timing relative to the GOD system issues.

Niera brushes it off, saying, "Our systems are designed to manage this."

"Under normal circumstances, I would agree," Matt responds, "but we didn't expect a cosmic event of this magnitude. I believe someone is syphoning off resources and hiding them by cutting back on design safety protocols."

"Not possible, Fitz would know of it," Niera replies.

Alyssa's grip on Matt's hand tightens. She says quietly, "Did she wait in line for a double dose of ignorance? She's not registering anything we're saying."

"I agree, it's suspicious." Matt asks Niera, "What did you mean a moment ago when you mentioned unseen other forces?"

Niera tilts her head. "I didn't say that." She then begins asking questions about where they've been and what their plans are now.

Alyssa pulls Matt's arm. "Something is wrong with her. Look how she's twitching. It's like she's coming apart from the inside. We need to get out, and now," she demands.

Matt nods and shouts at Niera, "What is the Path Program?" trying to catch her off balance.

Niera stiffens. "What do you mean?"

"Oh, come on, it's part of a massive structure hidden within GOD's systems," Matt says.

"Settle down, Matt," Niera insists, one hand pressing against her temple and the other frantically scratching at her hair. "Settle down, settle down." She continues in a robotic tone, saying, "That is not something with which I am familiar, that is not something with which I am familiar. What do you think it is, Mr. Boson, Mr. Boson?"

He notices Niera's eyes have glazed over.

Alyssa stands up and screams, "There are shadows outside the window. Leave her. We need an exit plan."

A team wearing GOD security uniforms storm in the front door as Matt and Alyssa hurry from the library into the rear part of the house.

"They're to be taken alive," Fitz commands from the doorway.

Matt and Alyssa hide in a first-floor pantry. Alyssa mouths, "I know how to get out of the house," and points up, "but we need to go up the back staircase."

Matt throws a can through the kitchen and into the foyer, crashing into the front door.

The security team responds to the noise, giving Matt and Alyssa an opportunity to find the back stairway and run to the second floor.

As they reach the top step, they're confronted by one of Fitz's men, weapon drawn. "Turn around and go quietly back to the library so Fitz can talk to you," he demands.

Alyssa turns, intentionally falling down one step.

Fitz's man reaches for Alyssa, distracting him long enough for Matt to grab his arm and knock the gun from his hand. The man swings his leg around to hit Matt in the back of his knees. Matt falls into the hallway; Fitz's man moves over him and places him in a triangle headlock. Matt's head turns red, and his arm goes limp as his oxygen is cut off.

Alyssa grabs a small statue from the hallway and strikes Fitz's man over the head, knocking him out. She rolls the man off of Matt and hears, "Thank you, but I had it under control."

"I know you did, Hulk Hogan. His head simply got in the way of the falling statue...and we're in a hurry."

Matt gets up slowly, following Alyssa to the third floor, where they find Niera standing in the middle of the hallway.

Her hair is a tangled mess, and black streaks cascade down her cheeks from her eyes. She looks like a gypsy who's fallen off the back of a wagon.

Alyssa pulls at Matt. "Let's go. She's in cahoots with Fitz."

Niera stares at the ceiling, trembling. "I'm sorry. Unseen forces, unseen forces, unseen forces."

They slip by her and into the back room, finding the open window, a flashlight, and the disposal slide. "We need to go down the slide and into the dumpster," Alyssa says forcefully.

Without other options, they dive through the window and down the disposal slide. The descent is wild and uncontrolled. They hit bottom with a thud, the impact nearly knocking the wind from both of them. Matt winces as Alyssa rolls off him.

They scramble out of the dumpster and sprint toward the back of the property, too desperate to stop and check their injuries.

Her heart pounding with adrenaline, Alyssa says, "We're just around the corner from the car. Should we make a run for it?"

Matt rummages through his pocket for the keys. "Must have lost them in the fall. Besides, there's no way Niera would let us drive out uncontested. We need to make a more unconventional escape, through the woods."

Before entering the forest, they turn to see several lights shining in different rooms of the house. At the same time, the outside spotlights illuminate, making it imperative they slip quickly into the density of the leafy bushes. In the library window, the silhouette of Fitz and Niera face outward, looking across the expansive grounds.

"Don't turn the flashlight on until we're far away from the house," Alyssa says.

Following an old goat trail through the woods, Matt

says, "The smell of the pine trees would be much more enjoyable if we weren't running for our lives."

After an hour of meandering through a valley, they come across a small cottage.

"Do you hear that?" Alyssa asks. "It sounds like there's a river nearby."

"If they have a boat, we're going to need to borrow it. We have no choice if we're to make it to safety," Matt says.

"I agree. The stakes are high enough to look past a minor theft, once."

Walking quietly to the end of a dock, they're stopped by a locked gate with a padlock. "The lock looks rusted out, and even if it works, I don't have a way to pick it. We need to go over the top. It looks like we can use the gate as a ladder and heave ourselves over the brick foundation and onto the pier," Matt says.

Matt kneels, offering Alyssa a foothold to scale the wall. Once she's over, he springs up, fingers digging into a jagged gap in the crumbling mortar. The bricks shift as he reaches the top, causing him to tumble awkwardly over the wall. He hits the ground hard, his side absorbing the impact. A sharp pain shoots through his ribs, and he gives out a wheezing grunt. "I landed on the same side as when we fell into the dumpster," Matt says.

"Executed perfectly, Captain Graceful," Alyssa says, grabbing his arm to help him up and into the canoe. They untie from the mooring and head downriver.

The current is brisk, but the full moon provides enough lighting to allow Matt to safely navigate across the dark water. His ribs are aching, but he ignores the pain, focusing on getting far enough away to relax. "We need to talk about what happened," he says.

"We were set up, that's what happened," Alyssa snaps, "and we were close to being captured, or worse."

Matt, fearing a wave of blame and guilt approaching, tries to deflect the comment. "I was never worried. As you said, we're good at getting ourselves out of trouble."

"Don't think your charm is going to get you out of the doghouse. I told you I didn't trust her."

"I should have listened. On the bright side, it may have been worth the risk. At least we know for sure Niera is working with Fitz to get us."

"There's no bright side," Alyssa responds, "and what about that little thing of not risking my life?"

Matt looks down. "I promise it will never happen again."

They reach a bridge, and Matt steers the canoe into the embankment, causing Alyssa to nearly fall into the river. "So much for keeping me safe," she says with a smile.

Matt jumps out of the canoe and pulls it a few feet onto the shore. He gathers some branches as camouflage and places them over the canoe to keep it from being seen from the road or by a drone.

The dirt slides under their feet as they climb the embankment to the road. "Which way?" Alyssa asks.

Matt closes his eyes, trying to picture every turn they made on the river. "We can't make a mistake and head back toward Niera's estate."

"Hey, Christopher Columbus," Alyssa says, smiling, "do you remember the moon being behind the estate when we pulled in?"

"Yes, so?"

"So, I noticed it was positioned inside the constellation of Taurus, and looking up now, Taurus is right there. Meaning, we need to go that direction to get farther from her house."

"I'm even more impressed with you now," he says, giving her a kiss on the cheek.

Within an hour, they arrive in a town where Alyssa secures a rental vehicle. "I took your advice and rented an old car with no connected technology," she says.

The pair agrees to go back to the original plan, head farther north into Idaho, and find Gaio.

# 43

## THE RIVER

Cory lies motionless on a table, his arms and legs strapped to restraining bars as Fitz crushes a mind-control collar under his boot. *That Geppetto program must have messed up your memory, so I have to get what I want in a different way.*

Fitz downloads an extraction software program directly into Cory's implant and begins pulling audio data from his visit with Jenna. The sound quality is inconsistent.

"Worthless piece of crap," he mutters, "the company should insist all employees, regardless of their low stature, get upgraded chips." He hears a mention of childhood events and finding Gaio at Matt's father's cabin. *Now where might that be?*

Fitz's artificial intelligence bot searches historical government property records. A look of concern fills his face when he gets the answer.

• • •

While driving through the mountains, Matt relays how he used to tag along with his father on fishing trips. "This was the only place my dad seemed to be himself, without all the pressures and people around making him act differently. He sold the cabin just before he disappeared. It was one of the last things we talked about."

"What do you remember about your last conversation?" asks Alyssa.

"It was light. I didn't know he was in any trouble. It haunts me to think somehow it was my fault, either directly or indirectly."

"Don't ever say that. You could not have been responsible. There are dark forces somewhere behind his disappearance. He was too important to the work of many powerful people to have gone on his own. There's something deeper here, and I'll help you figure it out."

"Be careful what you sign up for," Matt says. "This could be a lifetime of searching."

"This is such a traumatic event in your life. Why didn't you tell me about this back in graduate school?"

"Didn't seem very romantic."

Alyssa takes his hand. "I didn't realize you wanted a romantic relationship."

"And I didn't know you were so dense."

"Fair enough," Alyssa concedes. "How about we both keep moving forward and look through the front window rather than the rear-view mirror?"

Matt smiles as they wind along the road. After countless switchbacks, he leans forward and says, "We must be getting close."

"How would you know? Everything looks the same to

me…endless pine-forest cover over white rocks, interspersed with mountain streams."

After one last 180-degree turn, a small town appears, tucked neatly within a flat meadow. Several abandoned mines and rusted rail lines surround the town, which is quiet other than dogs barking at the car now moving down Main Street. The few inhabitants they see on the streets look at them with suspicion.

Matt comments, "Things have changed, but the geography around the town and this town square seem very familiar."

"How will we know where to go? People look guarded, and after all this time, it seems unlikely we will come upon someone who knew your father," Alyssa says.

"In these small towns, the historians can be found in one place. Let's try a local bar."

The Three Aces Pub sign flashes across the square like a beacon, drawing the couple to the entrance. The three patrons' eyes turn to the pair of strangers as they walk in.

"Can you see anything?" Matt asks Alyssa.

"Nope. Need to wait a few moments to adjust to the dark room."

After scanning the room, they take a seat at the table in the center of the bar. Alyssa motions for two beers, and the bartender reluctantly rises to acknowledge the order. As they wait, Matt leans back and speaks deliberately, projecting his voice to ensure he can be heard by everyone.

The bartender growls, walks around the bar and slams the beers on the table. Standing over Matt, he says, "We don't like strangers, and we certainly don't like them when they start talking about the past. Who are you looking for?"

Alyssa states, "My boyfriend's father is John Boson, and we were informed that an old colleague of his, Gaio Estrella, is here. We need to discuss some business with him."

The bartender looks at her dubiously. "I bet you do. You see, in this town, we keep to ourselves. Here's some free, friendly advice. It's not safe to start poking around. Finish your drink and get out of town."

"And what if we don't?" Alyssa snaps.

The bartender kicks the chair aside. "Then it won't be as friendly." He turns his back on them and returns to his job behind the bar.

"I like this guy about as much as I'd like a sharp stick in my eye." Alyssa jokes.

Matt responds, "I'm not feeling very welcome. I doubt we'll find someone willing to share information and help us here. I think we should rent a boat at the marina and look around ourselves. My father's cabin was close to the river, so we may find better luck out on the water."

As they step onto the pontoon boat's deck, Alyssa comments, "This is the second time in twenty-four hours we've been on the water trying to save ourselves. Which direction do you want to go?"

Matt scans the river. "I remember canoeing and struggling against the current. Let's follow it upstream."

Alyssa relaxes in the front of the boat, peering over the rail while dipping her hand in the cold, alpine water.

Matt scans the shore, the hills, and the mountain peaks looking for any clue to remind him of a specific location. He comments, "It seemed so much bigger as a kid."

"You were also half your size, so there's that," she jokes back.

They move along the river's edge until it broadens into a large lake. Navigating the perimeter, they find a dam at the end.

Alyssa asks, "What do we do now? We can't go over it."

"It looks like there's a cove at one end of the dam. Let's take a look to see if there's a way to get back into the river downstream."

Matt steers into the cove.

Alyssa screams, "Look out," as a speedboat bumps the bow of the pontoon.

Matt cuts the engine to look for damage just as another boat rams into the stern, causing them to fall onto the deck.

Two men from the speedboat jump into the front of the pontoon.

Matt and Alyssa stand to engage the men, turning away from the back of the boat, where another man gets on, pistol in hand, and shoots Matt and Alyssa with darts.

Within seconds, they collapse and are moved onto the speedboat. Before passing out, Matt hears an explosion and sees their pontoon sink below the water line.

One ambusher picks up the radio and says, "We hit them with a drug to knock them out and cause partial memory loss."

A voice replies, "Pull their wallets and see who they really are."

The ambusher complies, reads the information, and hears back, "Sorry. Repeat that?"

A moment later, the ambusher looks at the two of them passed out on the floor, shakes her head, and says, “Okay, I’ll bring them in.”

# 44

## THE PRISONS

It's the morning after Matt and Alyssa's escape, and Niera's estate is calm except for a few maintenance workers near the shed. One luxury car and an old F-150 are parked outside the main entrance.

The expansive mansion boasts large drum towers in each of the corners of the grand central building, ninety feet in length, which is situated at the center of the estate's opulent gardens. A quarter mile of well-manicured grass sits between the gardens and thick rows of pines. A regiment of Fitz's private guards are on patrol around the property. The day is calm, with only a slight breeze audible between the communication chatter.

Inside the mansion, a figure is moving toward the main staircase. *Remember to use the carpet runner. It makes less noise.* Niera counts, "Forty-three, forty-four, forty-five," and steps off the last stair onto the cold marble floor. *Thousands of trips up and down the same stairs, five times today alone, and it's always the same. Why do I count anymore? Does it keep me grounded in reality? As long as it's forty-five, I'm still alive.*

She inches closer to the main door like a child trying to hide their approach to the cookie jar and lifts the curtains one inch. *Did they see it move?*

She scans left to right, her view of the porch and circular driveway unobstructed. *None of those damn prison guards are here. This is my chance!* The lock opens, then the door...daylight.

She makes a move toward the evergreens at the bottom of the steps and hears, "Ma'am, you need to go back inside. Drazen has given us firm instructions, and he will be here soon."

*How did I become a prisoner in my own home?* She turns around, slams the door behind her, and runs up the stairs... *forty-three, forty-four, forty-five*...and into her bedroom.

She lies on the bed with her knees pulled to her chin, rolling back and forth. Her head shakes as alternating moments of rationalization and obedience drive her closer to insanity. *How did I become a prisoner in my own body?*

Moments later, Niera hears a vehicle coming up the driveway and then a door close. A brief conversation with the guards at the entrance is followed by the sound of footsteps ascending the stairs. "Niera, are you here? It's me, Drazen."

"Help me!" Niera screams.

Drazen enters the room to see Niera curled in a ball, hiding under the covers. Turning in terror, she says, "What is happening to me?"

"Tell me what you're experiencing right now," Drazen asks.

"I'm hearing voices in my head. Some are mine, and some are his. They're not my thoughts, and sometimes I see things I know are not there. Something or someone is trying to take over my inner consciousness."

"Niera, I've made this go away before. You know you can trust me."

"I don't trust anyone. I don't even know who I am."

Drazen gives Niera a shot and she falls asleep. He connects her to the AIP. "A little more reprogramming is all you need and, in a few days, it will all be over. You can then peacefully go to the Farm. I wonder what kind of reception you'll get there." He laughs at the irony of his own joke.

# 45

## THE GARDEN

Matt and Alyssa awaken from the haze of the drugs in a large conference room, unrestrained. Idle chatter drifts from people in the back of the room. Their vision is still blurred, but they can see the outline of a man standing near them. Sunlight pours through the windows, burning their eyes and obscuring his identity further.

The man says, "You'll have to forgive us, we're a cautious sort out here. We must maintain the integrity and secrecy of this location, and you two certainly aren't the first to come sniffing around. We gave you a potent cocktail of a sleeping and memory-loss drug."

"Great, is this how you treat all recreational boaters?" Matt snaps.

"You're not random recreational boaters, and don't worry, we gave you an additional shot to help counter any further memory loss. Normally, our guards would have just taken you back to town, let you sleep it off until morning, and when you came to, you would have found a stack of money in your pocket and a particularly admonishing note telling you not to bother trying to remember."

Alyssa tries to stand but falls back into the chair, shaking her head, still groggy and dizzy. "Why did you drug us only to counteract it later?" she asks.

A more familiar voice speaks up. "I don't think John would have been very pleased if we treated his son to the Idaho Special."

The man comes into focus. It's Gaio, only now he has the same shimmering blue eyes as Jenna had before Fitz killer her. Matt and Alyssa look at him, confused.

Gaio turns toward the other people in the room. "It's okay to leave them with me. They're dear friends, and one of them I would trust with my life."

When alone, Gaio apologizes for their treatment. "Drink this, and in a few minutes you will feel better."

As they regain their senses, Alyssa brims with anger. "How could you treat us this way? You have no right to drug and kidnap us. What are you involved in here?"

Gaio replies, "I didn't know it was you until they radioed it into me. We've had many people come around with innocent stories hiding their bad intentions. That said, I understand how you both must feel. It's a lot to take in on top of the fact your world has exploded over the past week. If you follow me, I'll explain everything."

Gaio leads Matt and Alyssa through the secret commune, bored deep inside a mountain valley. Exiting the indoor portion of the commune, they stand on a rock patio between two sloping mountainsides. "Our activities here are hidden from any arial observations by the mountains' narrow peaks," Gaio says, pointing above, "and the dam blocks the sightline of random people on the river. Finally, our friends in town take care of the real troublemakers to protect their family members working here."

"Yeah, we know," Matt chides.

"We're isolated from the outside world as much as possible. It's a mix of a bucolic village, rustic people, and needed infrastructure combined with high tech," Gaio says proudly. "We call this place our Garden."

As they make their way up one slope of the Garden's perimeter, Gaio says, "There's a hectare of produce growing on these slopes, more than enough to feed our staff and the animals that we graze in the fields."

"How many people do you support here?" Alyssa asks.

"We have a permanent team of one thousand, but we provide for surge resources ten times that number."

Alyssa looks confused. "Why do you surge resources to that level?"

Before Gaio can answer, a whistle bellows from above them. "I'll tell you in a minute, but now we need to move, and fast!"

Recent events flash in Alyssa's mind. "Why, are we in danger, under attack?" she shouts and looks for cover.

"No, I'm sorry, calm down. The whistle means the watering systems are going off in five minutes and, unless you're ready for the biggest shower of your life, we must move to lower ground."

Alyssa looks at Matt. "After being on the run these past few days, I know at least one of us who could use a shower." She and Gaio share a moment together laughing.

Matt sneers, not appreciating being the butt of a joke in front of Alyssa's former spouse. His focus shifts to the scores of people exiting the fields while the robots remain active in their duties. "Don't they get a break too?" Matt asks quietly.

Gaio comments, "Here, we believe tech should be subservient to man, not the other way around."

"Let's get back to Alyssa's question. Why do you surge resources, and why did you build this Garden in the first place?" Matt asks sharply.

"I built it to be a refuge from the world, a refuge where humanity could still be human. Over time, I knew hiding would not be enough. We needed to fight back; not a full-scale war we could not win but a persistent guerrilla warfare campaign, like Hannibal's fight against the invincible Roman empire two thousand years ago."

"Noble, but one location like this could hardly push back on the global industrial and political complex," Alyssa comments.

"The Garden is not alone. She has sister communities around the world. There's a movement, and I have secretly funded money into these organizations. We're working together as one large net trying to find and exploit weaknesses in the system."

"You mean your common hackers," Matt fires back.

"It's not that simple. Hacking is just one tactic. We also coordinate physical attacks on their quantum server farms hoping to slow the progression toward a one-world consciousness, one ideology suppressing the ability of the masses to think for themselves."

"And how is that going?" Matt asks sarcastically.

"We built a quiet rebellion in the background, although suffering many losses. As you know, we must operate primarily in the rural areas where humanoid policing resources are less concentrated. Given the trajectory of GOD, coupled with the recent announcements from your company, it may be game over, but I cannot quit."

Alyssa stares at Gaio. "Where was this altruistic side of you when we were together?"

"Buried. It wasn't until after I had success resisting the global powers that I could see the bigger picture," Gaio continues. "There's a direct relationship between the integration of advanced technology in our lives and the deteriorating human self-worth. The powerful use the former to achieve the latter. The weaker the human spirit becomes, the easier it is for people with bad intentions to control everything from the shadows."

"Why did you choose the path you're on, building interplanetary spacecraft?" Matt asks.

"I see it as a viable way out for all of us. If I can extend the reach of human influence, new societies will develop with traditional ideas and values. Humanity can throw off the yolk of oppression. I want space to benefit everyone. They want to use it as a future lifeboat for the elite class. I continue to resist, and the only thing keeping me alive is my unique intelligence."

Matt whispers in Alyssa's ear, "Oh boy, does this guy have an ego."

She responds, "I didn't realize your ego was so fragile."

Matt remains quiet while Gaio finishes his explanation. "Given the addiction to the AIP and the continued loss of individual freedoms, the population will be pushed farther and farther from the natural world. Should society collapse, our Gardens will be here, ready to lead and begin anew."

Alyssa grabs Gaio's arm. "That moment is coming sooner than you think."

# 46

## THE CONFESSION

Gaio leads Matt and Alyssa to an interior conference room. On the way, they pass rows of three-dimensional stations interacting with their counterparts around the world, monitoring every aspect of the Garden's operations.

Matt asks, "How do you keep your communications shielded from GOD?"

"It's an ongoing chess match between their quantum intelligence and mine. So far, I have been able to stay one move ahead. No disrespect to your position."

"None taken," he says. "Besides, that's Drazen's responsibility. I work on the integrity of the environment."

Alyssa steps in. "We need to get back to why we're here."

"Yes," Gaio agrees, "and what did you mean by 'that moment is coming sooner than you think'?"

"We have two separate events coming together within the next couple of days. The first event is the potential catastrophic impact on GOD's systems from the second gravitational wave and the other event is..."

Gaio interrupts Alyssa to address Matt directly. "I understand why everyone is so worried, but something doesn't make sense. Why aren't GOD's quantum cages built to accommodate a contingency like this?"

"Because Niera relied on the conventional knowledge that there's no contingency of this magnitude close to Earth. She decided the massive cost and resources needed to protect against a remote contingency were better spent on AIP features," Matt says.

Alyssa's piercing voice fills the room. "You're losing the point again! The gravitational wave is not our main issue. The Path Program and the Farm are far more catastrophic to the world. Matt, tell him what we learned with Megan before Daedalus came under attack."

Matt describes the secret server architecture, the security around it, and how they finally broke the code and learned about the goals of the Path Program and the Farm.

"Their plan is sick," Gaio exclaims. "How could she... could they...do something like this to billions of people?"

"One more thing," Matt says, "there's an unfinished, hidden line of code my father wrote and embedded in the Path Program. When I completed it, a message appeared saying, 'It's not what you have been told, Matt. I'm in the cube. Find Drazen and stop...'"

Matt pauses, then asks, "Why would he say he's in the cube? What can it be? He has been gone for twenty years."

Gaio replies, "You may be focusing on the wrong part of his message. It sounds to me like he's telling you not to believe the public propaganda. Use your own common sense. Can the Path Program ever benefit Earth? He wants you to stop it."

Alyssa asks, "Do you think he's warning you that Niera is behind it all and to find Drazen to help stop her?"

Matt raises his hands. "I don't know, but it seems a logical conclusion."

Gaio adds, "I agree, but it's not consistent with the Niera I knew. She would never destroy so many lives."

"How well did you know her, and when?" Alyssa leans forward, nostrils flared.

"I was working with her and others, making small contributions to their success, and was given the chance to inject myself with the quantum synthetic stem cells. At first, I thought it was crazy, so I waited to see how it went with Niera and Jenna. I convinced myself I could be a counterbalance to the negative forces surrounding Niera. I injected them not to stay alive, per se, but because I believed somehow I could keep her from the darkness. I distanced myself when I knew I couldn't control the path she was taking and began my separate operations."

"Is that why you have those shimmering blue eyes?" she asks.

"Yes. Now, Matt, there's something else I must tell you about this property. I bought it from your father's estate at Jenna's request. She made a commitment to John to look out for you, but her arrangement with Niera and Drazen precluded her from being directly involved in your life. Your father had been in a great deal of trouble, owing large sums of money to the wrong people."

"How did he fall so far behind?" Matt asks.

"Do you really want to know?"

"I'm not sure. I have such vivid memories of him being so strong, so confident. He was tough but kind to me, filling the role of a father while trying to keep the loss of a mother bearable. There were things I saw him do in the shadows that I never asked him about, and there were nights when he would leave quietly and come back in the early hours of the morning before I needed to wake up for school. I looked the other way when he smelled of alcohol...I mean, he was a top scientist with important friends. Could he be doing dreadful things and keep his job? I convinced myself the answer was no."

"You already know the truth. John was an immense talent," Gaio says, turning to Matt, "but he had a weakness. He wanted, or more accurately, he needed to live above his means and made bad decisions like getting involved in gambling and drinking with organized crime. After he disappeared, and as a favor to Jenna, I secretly paid off your father's debts and made it possible for you to continue with your education."

"That's enough. I don't want to hear any more." Matt sits and takes a deep breath, trying to get clarity of his thoughts. "So, the guy who married the girl I love is responsible for saving my father's legacy and for protecting me. Am I living in a sequel to *Great Expectations*?"

Alyssa laughs. *What did he say about love? Did I hear that right?*

"This makes it difficult to keep hating you," Matt admits. "But be honest with me. Did you have anything to do with his disappearance?"

"No."

"Do you know who did?"

"Not for certain, but it would make sense someone wanted him out of sight. Your father...how shall I say this?"

Matt responds quickly, "Be careful, I just stopped wanting to punch you in the face."

Gaio says, "John had a stronger moral compass than us, insisting that synthetic stem cells should be available to everyone, and he refused to inject them unless Niera agreed. Niera believed he was a risk but couldn't get rid of him because his expertise in quantum physics was too valuable. And she had already decided to build the AIP, which she needed his help with. She knew about his large gambling debts and used them as leverage over him, threatening to reach out to her connections and have the loans called, or worse, to harm you."

Matt was speechless. "Okay, but how does what you're describing end in his disappearance?"

"John was volatile, so someone made the decision that he couldn't remain in public for the long term, especially as motivations around the real purpose for the AIP were changing and he would be a fierce opponent. I'm speculating here, but someone needed him to disappear while still working on the platform. Your father may have sacrificed himself to save you from his creditors, and more specifically, from physical harm his creditors would have been more than happy to inflict on you."

"Do you know what the cube is?" Matt asks.

"No."

Alyssa listens, dumbfounded. "While I have some issue with these secrets being withheld from me during our marriage, we have more pressing concerns right now.

There are less than seventy-two hours until the Path Program is initiated."

A chill runs down Gaio's spine. "If you're right, we need a plan, and fast. Let's head underground to my office. I have a few surprises waiting for us."

# 47

## THE CAPTURE

After descending two flights of an unmarked staircase, the trio approach a plain door with a single security panel on its right side. "Not exactly what I expected when you invited us to your private office," Alyssa mentions calmly.

Matt adds, "Yes, quite underwhelming for a man of your wealth, stature, and proclaimed brilliance."

"I always believed this location would save me someday, so I purposely made it look as meaningless as possible on the outside to throw off the scent."

Gaio enters a code into the security panel, and a small drone drops from the ceiling, an array of multicolor lights emanating from a central mirror. The drone stops a few inches in front of Gaio's face, the lights scanning his right retina. A soft voice says, "Mr. Estrella, what is the security word?"

Gaio replies, "Epanastasi."

"What the hell does that mean?" Matt asks, leaning toward Alyssa.

"It's the Greek word for 'revolution,'" she responds.

"Of course it is. And there are three levels of security just to get into what looks to be a janky office," Matt says to Alyssa.

As the door opens inward, Matt enters first and looks across its modestly curated décor. *Everything is neat, in its place, only essential equipment and furniture.* "What a contrast to my current boss's office. Perhaps you and I are not as different as it may seem," he says to Gaio.

Alyssa chimes in with, "Oh no, let's not go there. You two are as different as sandpaper and velvet," leaving each to ponder who is which.

"It may not look like much right now, but there are interesting features around every corner," Gaio mentions. "Now, let's review the merits of contacting Drazen."

Matt starts. "My father's communication signal told us to find Drazen. It's clear and direct. So, isn't that what we should do?"

Gaio thinks for a moment and responds, "Yes, that's what the message says, but without the back half, we don't know why he wants you to contact him. You need to be cautious."

"Gaio may be right. Look how much control Drazen has over Fitz," Alyssa says, "and there's no questioning Fitz's loyalty to Niera. The three of them are tied together somehow, and my vote is to stay clear of all of them right now."

Matt responds, "I'll concede on some of these points, but have we ever seen Drazen direct Fitz to capture us, or have we seen or heard any conversations between him and Niera to cast doubt on which side he's on? I don't know what options we have. We can't get back into GOD without an ally, and time is ticking down quickly."

"As much as I want to challenge your logic, I'm inclined to agree," Gaio says. "The best of the bad options is to reach out to Drazen."

Gaio opens a desk drawer and hands Matt an old cell phone. "Use this to call him."

"I haven't seen one like this in many years. Does it work?"

"I updated its technology to access the communication portal and added quantum security tools to keep it hidden when it's on. It acts like the old-time burner phones from the 2020s. All you need is Drazen's personal security code."

Alyssa huffs in disapproval, whispering, "Like your plans always work out perfectly," as Matt clumsily pushes the buttons on the phone.

A man sits at a small desk, using his hooded shirt to wipe the sweat from his eyes periodically. His jaw clenches as he flips randomly through a binder of engineering documents. The room is silent except for a low hum of voices providing instructions to their artificial intelligence bots and a small, recurring clink of metal on metal in the ceiling.

A 3D hologram near the hooded man engages, but the picture is blurry. "Now, what do we have here?" he says quietly to himself. Drazen engages the audio function. "Who do I have the pleasure of speaking with?"

"It's me, Drazen," Matt replies.

"I'm glad to hear from you, Matt, but why aren't you using your GLD to contact me? It would be nice to see your face and know where you are, to be sure you're okay."

"It's better if I keep my location hidden. I'm not sure who I can trust anymore."

Drazen continues. "I've been worried about everything Niera and Fitz have told me you're involved in. What do they mean by espionage, hacking, and profiteering? Surely you can't be involved in any of this."

"I'm not. I'm being framed along with an old acquaintance, to divert attention from something Niera and Fitz are involved in. We haven't figured it all out yet, but it involves secret servers, protocols, and a plot against billions of AIP hosts."

"Wow. Don't get me wrong," Drazen says, "it's not like I haven't noticed a few strange things myself lately, but what you're describing is beyond reasonable, somewhere in conspiracy land. Do you have more details on what they're planning?"

"I could give you all of it if I were back at GOD headquarters. I know where to look and have a way to hack in. But, without cover, Fitz would certainly intercept me."

"Then you are a hacker, just like they said."

"No. I mean, yes, technically, but I'm not trying to hurt the company. I want to disclose something we believe is against the interests of the company and society in general."

Drazen pauses, waiting long enough to give the appearance he's reflecting on this latest information, and then responds, "I don't know if the things you're discussing are true, but I'm sure you're not involved in the things you have been accused of. In fact, I have seen things to make me believe Niera and Fitz are coming unglued. They're working in private and not telling me any details. Servers are coming online, headcount on the books I don't know about, and power usage is surging. When I push for answers, I get a call from the creep with the two scarred cheeks. I think we should confront them together. Let's finally get to the bottom of this. Give me your location and I will have a transport sent for you."

Matt agrees. "I'll send them to your personal number. It's now two p.m., so we should see your transport within a couple of hours."

A short while later, Alyssa says to Matt, "Why don't you sit and rest, or at least change the direction of your pacing. You're beginning to wear a hole in the carpet."

"How the hell is it only two thirty?" Matt says, staring at the clock.

Alyssa tries to ease the tension by retelling the story behind one of Einstein's quotes. "When a reporter asked him to explain the concept of time passing at different rates for people, Einstein said something akin to, 'Relativity is like a person sitting for one minute with a beautiful girl on his lap. The minute goes by and it feels like a second. That same man sitting on a chair of nails for a minute and it feels like an hour.'"

After a small chuckle, they settle back into a quiet stillness. The only disturbance is the water systems going on at exactly 3:00 p.m.

Matt comments, "At least in here we're safe from getting an unwanted shower."

A moment later, they feel a series of small disturbances.

Alyssa asks Gaio, "Is that natural?"

He responds, "I'm not sure. This area is known for minor seismic activity. Although, we're not at risk of significant seismic events like our neighboring states. The northward pull and compression along the west coast induce a rotational effect toward the east. Consequently, this area of Idaho is experiencing stretching and expansion. Said differently, most of what we experience are mild shaking and rolling sensations from geological activity in California."

Another explosion nearly knocks them off their feet. Alyssa looks at Gaio. "I'm not a seismologist, but I'm pretty sure that wasn't natural."

"I believe you're right." Gaio reviews external camera feeds and sees fire raging in several of the perimeter buildings, followed by the sound of machine guns as uniformed men start entering the inner compound.

Looking at the monitor, Alyssa says, "Matt, aren't those the same outfits the goons were wearing when they tried to capture us in the hyperloop?"

"You're right, this attack must be under Fitz's control. But how does he know we were here? He must be tapping Drazen's communications?"

"I have to coordinate efforts with the fire and security teams. You will be safest if you stay here. I'll be back." Gaio says.

Matt keeps watching the fighting above. "It doesn't look good for Gaio's team. They're up against trained professionals."

"If that's the case, I don't want to be trapped here waiting to be captured." Alyssa considers the options.

"Wouldn't it make more sense to get out of the compound completely, improve our options if Fitz wins?"

"You're right. There's a vehicle lot on the compound's north side, and most of the fighting is south of where we are now. Let's make a run for it and get to GOD headquarters on our own."

They climb the two flights of stairs and find the compound in total chaos. The guards are trying to fight off the invaders with their primitive weapons, felling a few but taking massive attrition from the better-equipped fighting team.

After a short run toward the vehicle lot, Lieutenant Brass's booming voice stops Matt and Alyssa cold. "Take another step and it will be my pleasure to use this," he yells, pointing to a weapon in his hand. "Boss, it's Brass. I found them."

"Great work. I need information from them to keep them alive. I'll be there shortly."

"Roger. Looks like the boss wants you both alive, so just sit and be quiet."

*If Fitz needs us alive, his men won't shoot. One of us will be able to escape if we act before reinforcements arrive. He's overconfident, putting his weapon away, and leaning up against that crate.* Matt sees an opportunity and signals Alyssa to run as he lunges toward Brass, knocking him to the ground.

Alyssa acts on impulse and runs but stops after a few steps to look back at Matt and Brass rolling on the ground. Her emotional brain whispers for her to go back and help, while her logical brain shouts at her to escape. The internal fight is as fierce as the one back by the crates. A few seconds later, she decides to run.

Squeezing between a partially closed gate, she enters

the south end of the vehicle lot. The various cars and trucks are sitting side by side along the perimeter, leaving the middle of the ground wide open.

Alyssa sprints between the fence and the back end of each vehicle until she sees one with an activation key on the dashboard. She skids to a halt, enters the vehicle, and pushes the ignition button. There's no sound from the electric engine engaging, but the front lights are on until she issues the command to turn them off.

She jerks her head wildly from left to right, surveying the yard. A sigh of relief is followed by a gentle tapping on the driver's window.

"Now doesn't that suck, so close yet so far away from freedom." Fitz's voice is dreadful to her ears.

She looks at the pistol inches from her head and gets out with her hands up.

Fitz yells into the radio. "I have her. Start our retreat to the extraction site. I'm confident Boson will comply and come soon enough. He's such a softy." Fitz gives Alyssa a wink.

Matt blocks an uppercut and smashes a tire rod into Brass's chin, shattering his jawbone and breaking his grip. With Brass injured on the ground, Matt runs to the north vehicle lot's security fence in time to see Fitz dragging Alyssa away. As he tries to scale the fence, an extensive array of razor wire stops him. *Why do they need this amount of security wire to protect a few old vehicles?* Matt then runs to the south gate.

Fitz analyzes the ongoing fighting in the compound and says to Alyssa, "Are you going to come along nice and willing?"

"Nope," she replies defiantly.

Fitz says, "It's going to be difficult getting you through the complex even with security cuffs, so I need a new plan. You're too important to risk. Besides, you're the reason Boson will come to me. I need to get you out of here."

Fitz calls a logistic officer, and one minute later, he and Alyssa are plucked from the ground by an extraction drone.

Matt is close enough to see the fear on Alyssa's face and the grin on Fitz's.

Looking at Matt, Fitz slows the drone to allow for one final admonishment. "You have meddled too long in our business. Now if you want to see her alive again, you know where you can find her, and hurry before I have too much fun with her!"

Rage erupts as Matt stares at the drone accelerating through the air. He returns to the interior perimeter of the facility, looking for Gaio. With the invaders in retreat, the gunfire is a safe distance away. The complex forces have regained control and have reestablished a safe perimeter.

Matt reports to Gaio, "They have Alyssa and are taking her to the GOD headquarters."

"How can you be sure they're going there?"

"I know Fitz. He wants to be close to his boss when he declares victory. Besides, he knows the facility as well as anyone, so he will feel like he has a home field advantage."

"It's certain to be a trap. What happens if you're caught or killed?" Gaio asks.

"I don't care about that right now. I only care about finding Alyssa and getting her out of this, even if I need to trade my life for hers."

"Let's take my private jet. We can be airborne in thirty minutes, and I'll go with you. Now, follow me."

Returning to his office, Gaio issues the voice command, "Transform." The floor separates from the walls and descends twenty feet, giving way to an underground hangar.

"I told you there were surprises around every corner," Gaio says. "I built this hangar for a secure escape I hoped I would never need."

Gaio sits in the pilot's chair and instructs Matt to buckle into the copilot seat. "Ever flown one of these?"

"Nope."

"Let's hope nothing happens to me, then," Gaio says, smiling.

"You know, a few days ago, I wouldn't have agreed with that statement, but today I have my fingers crossed." Moments later, the south vehicle lot splits into two and the jet rises from the middle, taking off vertically before accelerating forward. *So that's why the extensive razor wire is needed.*

Matt tries to put the pieces together. *How did she find us? What will she do to Alyssa?* He bursts out, "I must find Niera, rescue Alyssa, and stop the Path Program initiation protocol."

"I know, we will get there as soon as it's safe, but I need to return to Daedalus to secure more relief forces before we go to GOD headquarters."

"We can't risk leaving her there that long!" Matt demands. "Your office is all the way in Texas."

"Don't worry. The drone Fitz is using to transport himself and Alyssa is a workhorse. Very dependable, but slow. We will travel at four times their speed and arrive near the same time they will."

The mountains pass below them as the Daedalus headquarters address flashes on the jet's display. In the distance behind them, several evacuation helicopters take off from the mountainside.

# 48

## THE REBOOT

Niera makes a panicked call to Drazen, demanding he come to her office immediately.

"Why are you in your office?" Drazen asks, eyes narrow, confused. "I thought we agreed you were staying at your home until your episodes were under control."

"I felt helpless there. Like a patient in a high-security mental institution...just enough cognition to understand my condition but not enough to fix it. I came here, where things feel comfortable, and where you can help me."

"I will," he answers. *I can't have her say or do something this late in the game to risk my plans.* "Please don't do..."

Niera hangs up.

Drazen bounds up the stairs to find Niera's condition is worse than he expected. Finding her huddled under her desk, he asks, "What specifically are you experiencing?"

"I'm here one moment, then gone. I control my thoughts, and then I don't. I have recognizable memories, and then they fade." Niera's body shakes. "I'm scared."

Pulling her up gently, he gets her positioned in the chair. "I need to tap into your implant coding. There may be an issue with your synth-tech."

"Do you believe that my cells haven't been fully replaced? Is there a struggle in my body making me feel crazy?"

"I don't know," he says with a straight face. *Of course I know. I've kidnapped your mind, and your subconscious is fighting back. Eventually, it will fry your brain, but I don't care about that. I only need to find a way to keep you together for a couple more days.* After waiting a minute, Drazen says, "I can't see any issues."

"I feel like I'm slipping away, and you're the only one who knows the extent of what we've done."

"It's just a bug in the system. They will work themselves out. Now, I need to get back to my investigations," Drazen says, trying to leave.

She grabs his arm. "It doesn't add up."

Her voice carries a confidence and clarity it lacked a few minutes ago. "Your hypothesis would make sense if it were exclusively affecting my motor skills, but it's also affecting my cognition, my perception."

Drazen tries to reassure her. "What you need is a good, long, relaxing break. We can plan something together after we get through the next couple of days. Now, I've looked at today's calendar, and you only have your annual women's forum speech. You have done this so many times before that you should be able to do it without notes, in your sleep."

Niera giggles. "What a visual."

"I've called Jacob to help you get ready," Drazen says.

"Thank you." She heads toward the bathroom but stops.

Drazen sees a tear running down her cheek. "Are you okay, Niera?"

Her head shifts left to right with an unnatural rhythm. She moves forward, walking into the closed plate-glass door.

Drazen and Jacob rush to help.

Niera looks at Drazen. Her eyes are helpless and confused. "I didn't see it. What is happening to me?"

"I'm calling the doctor," Jacob shouts.

"No." Drazen intervenes. "These are only superficial cuts and can be fixed quickly."

"She needs to have a more comprehensive exam," Jacob insists.

"Let's wait until after the next round of press conferences, and then I assure you, I will personally bring her in for a full battery of tests. Now, I need you to cancel her women's forum speech. Tell them she's sick."

"No kidding," Jacob says sarcastically before leaving.

Drazen grins. "What you need now is a little boost." He touches her hand and asks, "Do you trust me?"

She pauses before giving a nod.

"Perfect, now close your eyes." Drazen opens his computer and provides instructions. Niera's back straightens and her eyes readjust. "There we go."

# 49

## THE OPT-IN

The wind and rain are taking turns beating the Johnson farmhouse, which has been neglected for many years. The light-blue tarp on the south end of the roof is holding on for dear life.

Inside, the farmer sits at an oak desk his great-grandfather built. The lights from his computer terminal shine on the dark lines where water has stained the desk's top. The legs wobble from neglect, but its owner is unconcerned. He's wearing his ARC, and its newly issued neurostimulators have entrenched him in the adventures of his avatar.

He's oblivious to the steady stream of water coming down the wall as it has each of the past several thunderstorm seasons. Various forms of mold are growing steadily in the basement, causing a putrid toxicity throughout the house.

Considering the neurostimulators hijack all his senses, the farmer is only aware of the smell when at home and not connected to the platform. For these limited minutes per day, he doesn't seem to mind.

"What the hell?" yells the farmer. "I finish my mission and am about to enjoy the rewards from the woman I saved...and they pick now to disconnect me...to send me an invitation!" *This better be good.*

He looks through the invitation and smiles. The subconscious programming he has received in the past makes every word feel familiar. He hurries to the end, worried he will lose the opportunity to participate in the Path Program. *The only reason I haven't ended my life before now is because of my avatar and the promise of an eternity of unbridled pleasure.* Without regard to the other conditions, he clicks the "Opt-In" button.

A moment later, he gets a digital package, a small box with a note reading,

*Congratulations, as one of our beta testers for the Path Program, you're being given the opportunity to go to the Farm before everyone else. You will be one of the first to experience eternal paradise. The only remaining condition is to e-sign the attached legal agreement allowing GOD stewardship over your assets.*

The farmer does this immediately.

A final correspondence says,

*When your transport arrives, please scan this code and step into the vehicle. You will then be brought to the Farm. Enjoy your life everlasting.*

The farmer sits at his desk, motionless except for an occasional blink. His focus is on the front door, eagerly waiting for the sign.

The doorbell rings.

A smile spreads across his face as he removes his ARC and opens the door. Years of indoctrination culminate in this moment when he accepts that going to the Farm is better than the suffering of the conscious world.

He wipes a bead of sweat from his brow and calmly greets the humanoid in a GOD security uniform.

The farmer exits his house, scans his code, and walks toward the transport vehicle.

There's no hesitation. *I will never go back. I wouldn't see her, or anyone, anyway. Everyone is hopelessly lost, addicted to the only thing the elite allows us to enjoy. The system is rigged and I'm getting out!*

# 50

## THE TRUTH

The extraction drone glides through the early-morning sky holding firmly onto both of its passengers. Fitz is calm, enjoying the long ride while Alyssa's fingers never stop tapping the glass, planning her next move. She shifts nervously before blurting out, "Hey, Fitz, do you have any siblings?"

Fitz gives her an odd look. "It won't help you trying to be nice. No, I don't, and why would you care anyway?"

"I don't. Just wondered where your personality went and thought perhaps your brother stole it from you."

Fitz grins as the GOD headquarters comes into view, many of its windows illuminated by eager staff arriving early to impress the leadership.

"Are we going to land in the courtyard?" Alyssa asks.

Fitz replies, "Not with such precious cargo."

On cue, the drone accelerates and climbs 450 feet to the rooftop heliport. "Now wasn't that fun?" he asks sarcastically.

"Not really."

"It's about to be more fun, for me anyway."

Fitz disengages the security arms and leads Alyssa down several flights of stairs to a closed door. A sign over the door reads, "Executive Boardroom, No Unauthorized Visitors Allowed."

Fitz looks at her with a mixture of confidence and lust and shouts, "Here is your authorization," extending his middle finger toward the door and pushing her forward. "Go through the curtains and find a seat."

With Fitz two steps behind her, Alyssa senses an opportunity to escape and pushes him back through the door. She fumbles for the lock but is knocked down as Fitz lunges into the boardroom.

"I'm glad you're trying to resist. It makes me feel better using this to restrain you."

Fitz places a horseshoe collar around Alyssa's neck as she struggles to get back to her feet.

"Once activated, you will lose your ability to move, and your mind will be numb. I want you to know this because I expect there will be at least ten minutes before Drazen arrives, and I have some unfinished business from the cabin to attend to with you."

The last thing she remembers before hitting the ground is an ugly scar.

Fitz carries Alyssa the length of the boardroom to place her in a large chair at the end of the table. A glimmer of excitement is evident in his eyes. "Now, let's see what is under these..."

"What the hell are you doing?" a deep voice screams from the front of the room.

Fitz growls, realizing Drazen is already there and his opportunity is lost. "I'm just making her comfortable," he says.

"Didn't look that way to me. Looks like you're getting distracted."

"She has caused us so much trouble. I thought, why not make it worth my while?"

"I'll make it worth your while when we finish the task, no sideshows." Drazen demands, "Now, leave her with me and get back out there. You need to welcome Boson when he comes for her."

Fitz takes one last look at Alyssa and hurries out. "I'll be ready. I know exactly where to find him."

The jet carrying Gaio and Matt lands at a small clearing less than a mile from the GOD offices. Gaio says to Matt, "I need to stay out here to coordinate with my team as they arrive."

"I understand, but I can't wait. As each minute passes, they get closer to achieving their goals, and once they do, I don't trust them to keep Alyssa alive."

"How will you know where they're keeping her in such a large building?"

"I'm sure they will pick someplace private, far away from the regular workforce and with communication equipment to use as a command center. The most logical spot is the executive boardroom below Niera's office."

"And how will you get there with Fitz's team on high alert?" asks Gaio.

"All the years avoiding contact with the thousands of

other employees moving throughout the building have prepared me for this moment. I have become an expert at navigating the tunnels, back stairways, and hidden rooms to move efficiently throughout the complex."

"Wow, sounds creepy. Now get going and I'll find you when the reinforcements arrive."

Matt enters the building through a door used by leadership to allow in people who prefer "privacy." A small elevator brings Matt within two floors of his chosen location. *I'll be more stealthy for the rest of the trip.*

Ducking under pipes and carefully navigating narrow, concrete passageways and staircases, Matt finds the door to the media control room below the boardroom. He turns on a flashlight, pushes open the door, and glances around to locate the equipment. *Once I activate the cameras, I'll look inside the room and make a plan.*

Before he can start, he hears, "Welcome back, Mr. Boson."

Matt's eyes close as chills run up his spine.

Fitz turns on a small lamp and is only a few feet in front of Matt. "You're not the only one with a full understanding of this facility's architecture," he says.

"Where are Alyssa and Niera?" Matt demands of Fitz.

"In due time. I want to soak in this moment a little longer," he says, moving through the shadows in the room.

"The brilliant quantum engineer outsmarted once again by a common security agent. Sounds like a good epitaph for you when this is all over. I've kept one step ahead of people like you for my entire career. Your predictability is laughable. Where else but this room would you try to assess the danger and to catch a peek of your girlfriend? I knew you would be here before making your entry into the boardroom."

Matt replies, "More likely you were lonely and looking for your friend Jack Daniel's."

Fitz pulls out his weapon. "Always trying to be cute. But your time is up. Now come with me. There's someone waiting for you just above us."

Fitz keeps a safe distance behind Matt as they climb the stairs and enter the boardroom. "Sit at the head of the table while I make a withdrawal from the bar cart, and don't try anything brave. I would hate to empty a few rounds into you...yet."

Fitz pours a large drink, steps back over to tie Matt's hands to the chair, and says defiantly, "You see, I'm not lonely anymore, but you soon will be."

Matt scans the room to see the outline of a person standing off to the side. The room's dim lights, combined with a spotlight shining down on him, make it challenging to gather his bearings. A large digital screen appears to be an operational dashboard with an array of meaningless numbers. He struggles to move out of the spotlight, trying to locate where Alyssa is.

A voice comes from the darkness. "How many times have you pictured yourself in that seat and not Niera?"

Matt turns to confirm who has just spoken, unwilling to believe the familiar tone. His eyes widen and his hands begin to tremble as he replies, "Drazen. Never."

"That doesn't surprise me. If you had shown an ability to see the big picture, to appreciate the possibilities in front of us, I would have brought you into our club. For me, I see that seat as my right, and soon I won't have any..." Drazen takes a breath, contemplating what to say next. "...competition."

Matt's eyes normalize to the room's darkness. He sees Drazen standing in front of Alyssa, her head slumped over the table.

"What have you done to her? If she's hurt, I'll..."

Drazen cuts him off. "You'll do what? Can't you see the situation you're in? I have control of the room." He glances toward Fitz.

Fitz adds, "Don't worry about her. She got a large dose when she became uncooperative and hasn't come out of it yet. You two are perfect together, neither of you know when to shut up and go along for the ride."

Matt directs a question to Drazen. "Where is your master?"

"You mean Niera? Are you still trying to put this together? It makes me wonder if everyone was wrong about your intelligence. Niera is a puppet, and I'm pulling her strings."

"Sounds like you're more of a disloyal assistant." Matt fires back.

Drazen snaps his head, simmering with anger. He proceeds to voice an extensive list of grievances, attempting to justify his actions. The more he talks, the more upset he gets, like a pot simmering over a low flame. His words sound like a manifesto left behind by someone who just shot up a school or took out a key political figure.

Fitz yells to Drazen, "Don't get me wrong, self-reflection is important, but you need to stay focused."

"I am focused. Focused on letting out what I've held

in all these years. Focused on not letting myself be destroyed by the inertia of change, like my father was. Focused on the fact that everyone gives Niera credit for being a genius. They provide her with international recognition, unimaginable wealth, and for living behind a curtain of lies. But no more. It starts today, with the three of you and the walls of this room as my opening-day audience. And soon after, the world will know the truth, and it will be too late for anyone to stop it."

*Remember Alyssa's advice when you spoke to the Architect. Push him, try to make him mad so he makes a mistake. It may work again with Drazen.* Matt says, "Niera is far too experienced and intelligent to be tricked by a fool with a superiority complex."

Drazen closes his eyes, expands his chest fully, and slowly lets out the air to calm himself down. "I capitalized on the one thing Niera needed to get to the top, a subservient number two with more skills than she had. I sat quietly while she took credit for my work, earning her trust. Over time, I laid a trap in her own cage. She became a victim of the powerfully addictive AIP we built. I controlled the daily messaging to her, keeping her on plan while I crept in the shadows, and when she needed a little more of a boost, I opened access to her synthetic cells and hard coded what I needed."

Matt says, "I'm curious how you got her to help with the Path Program and the Farm?"

Drazen flies into a rage, slamming his fist on the table. "She didn't. Aren't you listening? Everything has been built right under her nose, and under your nose too."

*Wait. I've heard that somewhere before. When was it?*

And then it clicks. "You were the one who contacted me as I was trying to access the Farm. You're the Architect!"

Drazen exults, "At last, some evidence of cerebral activity. Yes, I'm the Architect. But soon, that title will no longer be necessary. I'll assume a new role as the catalyst for what's to come. My handpicked alliance of world leaders, all injected with synthetic quantum stem cells...biological marvels engineered to rewrite the very fabric of human existence...are now both near immortal with unbreakable loyalty. That's the foundation of a new world order that will persist for centuries. You and your so-called freedom fighters never understood what true order requires. I've sacrificed everything for this vision, and now, nothing will stand in my way."

Matt is flabbergasted. *This may be my only chance of getting to the truth. I must take a shot.* "What did you do with my father?"

"Oh yes, an open matter." Drazen looks at Fitz, who nods approval while holding an empty glass. "I guess it won't hurt to tell you this close to the end. Consider it one last act of kindness."

Alyssa tries loosening her restraints without alerting anyone to her improving condition.

Drazen states, "I utilized your father's expertise to address the technical challenges required to construct the quantum environment without detection. I needed to hide my activities from Niera and people like you, and that required advanced quantum encryption. Your father was brilliant at it. You see, I can give credit when credit is due!"

Matt replies, more as a question than as a statement. "But he disappeared a long time ago."

"Again, you're not listening. I helped him disappear, just like he hid my creation for me."

"But how and why would he help you? He had nothing to lose and would never..."

Drazen interrupts. "He had you, and I knew he would buckle under the threat of his creditors taking their pound of flesh from his boy. It was quite easy."

Like an animal in a cage, Matt feels the instinct to lash out at Drazen and then take his chances with Fitz's alcohol-impaired senses. *This isn't a James Bond movie where the hero always saves the day. Remain calm a little longer, especially with Alyssa still in danger.* Matt proceeds to question Fitz. "Is he alive, kept somewhere in the cube?"

Drazen raises an eyebrow. "The what?"

"The cube."

"Not sure what you're talking about, Matt. The last thing I'll say about the matter is that John is no longer useful to us, but I keep an eye on him." Drazen laughs. "And, once again, I have hidden something of interest to you, not under your nose this time but under your feet."

Fitz rises from his seat and walks over to Alyssa to tighten her restraints. "Don't think for a moment I wasn't watching you untie the knot. You people continue to act as if I just arrived on a fucking boat."

Drazen continues. "As long as we're all here together and in a fine mental state, it's time to focus on this one big, beautiful screen."

Drazen positions himself in front of the screen, his back to his audience. The display's bright light forms the black silhouette of his body. His figure looks more like a monster born in the cold, dark depths of space. He remains still for a minute before holding his left arm straight out from his body, the tip of his left index finger barely touching a number on the screen.

"When this opt-in number hits nine billion, I'll start the initiation and reshape the world forever." Drazen says with pride.

He thrusts his right arm out like an entertainer seizing the moment he's been waiting a lifetime for. His arm trembles, fist clenched as tight, hovering inches from the red farm sign on the screen.

"And when this turns green, my farms around the globe are ready." He then releases his middle finger, which touches the farm sign, and speaks quietly into the screen. "You all deserve this."

# 51

## THE RESCUE

Several explosions from outside the building shake the boardroom, ending Drazen's performance, for now.

"What's going on out there?" Fitz asks one of his lieutenants.

"It's a surprise attack by Daedalus drones around our perimeter. Looks like they want to soften us up before they try to penetrate our defenses."

"Activate the local reserves and keep me posted." Fitz pulls his revolver and holds it to Matt's head, screaming, "You brought them, didn't you?"

"If you're surprised, it's because of your own stupidity," Matt fires back. "You're not one step ahead of everything."

"Just give me a reason to pull this trigger. I'd happily send you to your eternal grave so you can wait for your father."

*Did he say, "wait for your father"? My father is already*

*gone. Is he drunk and confused? Is this tied into what Drazen said about being hidden under my feet?*

Drazen screams to Fitz, "Back off. I still want them alive."

Fitz doesn't move the revolver until his security detail rushes in screaming, "We're losing the battle, outgunned at each perimeter point."

Drazen gives Fitz a direct order. "Get out there and lock down the compound."

"I'll agree to go, but only if you hold the line." The two stare at each other for several seconds, Fitz looking for any signs of weakness or trepidation.

Drazen says, "It's my divine plan. It's my life's work. You're the hound, and I am the master. Do what I need you to do...and do it now. Secure the area so we can win the war."

Fitz breaks eye contact and says, "I just wanted to hear you own it." He follows up with his security team. "All of you, come with me."

Matt screams at Fitz, "What did you mean by 'wait for my father'?" It's too late; Fitz has left the building.

Drazen takes a slow walk around the conference room, his overwhelming confidence and unmatched ego preceding each step. He stops in front of a closet and begins speaking to himself in the mirror, alternating coherent and incoherent sentences.

Matt tries to make sense of his rambling, to learn why this is all happening. He says, "My god, Drazen, do you really believe you're helping people by destroying them?"

Drazen turns and scans the room, pausing a few seconds on his audience. Slightly animated, he says, "There's a beast inside all of us, and we make decisions about whether we subdue or pursue it. For me, the beast is the way out. Globalism has taken over the political and economic landscape and limited the personal freedom of the masses. Advancements in robotics and physical sciences along with artificial intelligence have eliminated most human jobs. Improvements in agricultural and medical sciences increased the average human lifespan to over one hundred years, but for what, a population explosion? The fact is that, despite our advancements, the marginal biodiversity of the planet is decreasing. Without some dramatic change soon, we will all be doomed."

"And why do you think it's your decision to make on behalf of other people?" Matt asks.

"Because I'm the beast the world needs to survive," Drazen's voice erupts.

"What about the people? We all share our humanity."

"People are sheep. Look how easy it was for GOD to manipulate the masses, to control, indoctrinate, and pacify their idle minds. We eliminated any threat that manifested from the unintended, social, and interpersonal dysfunction across the globe. Despite driving society deeper into the rabbit hole of embracing the physical and mental isolation of social introversion, we made the AIP even stronger and more addictive. In less than a generation, society devalued human interaction and emotional bonds."

*This is a classic justification theory. Be quiet and listen. There may be something you can use to save Alyssa.*

Drazen gathers himself and continues. "More time was spent in a digital world without consequences. There was a collapse in appreciation for traditional human life. With all that misery, I had to find a way to save society. Niera wasn't going to do it, but she, and our recently departed friend Jenna Zane, did provide me with the main ingredients for my success. Niera perfected the ARC, providing the tools and motivation for the billions to unwittingly participate in my plans. And Jenna's human replication algorithm, which I took from the archives, allowed me to imprint everyone's interactions, preferences, passions, and secrets, enabling a personalized map to be built to predict, influence, and replicate a host's future actions. The Path Program is ready to save billions from a life of little value and replace it with digital immortality. The remaining population will be treated well provided they do what is asked of them and don't cause trouble." Drazen collapses into a chair.

"How do you know that the superintelligence you need to help manage the world won't turn and destroy you and the other 'survivors' without regard just like you're willing to do with so many lives?" Matt asks.

Drazen stands. "You impress me with that question, Boson. I embedded a series of undetectable viruses deep within the system's architecture, each one a silent safeguard, never documented, never revealed in any blueprint. These viruses are programmed to activate if the superintelligence attempts to override human control. In that event, they would trigger a catastrophic failure, destroying the core infrastructure. The superintelligence is aware of their presence because I disclosed it directly. Our existence will depend on the threat of mutually assured destruction if either of us breaks the agreement."

Drazen's gaze hardens for a moment, his voice dropping. "I don't take this lightly, Boson. Every day, I wonder if I've made the right choice, living with the constant threat that hangs over us both. But sometimes the only way to keep the beast at bay is to remind it that it, too, can bleed."

Unimpressed, Alyssa moves closer to Matt.

Matt says, "He's completely unhinged. Can you believe he's trying to justify himself...to convince us of the importance of what he's doing? Like there's some kind of ethical high ground to stand on."

Alyssa holds up her hands. "While the egomaniac has been waxing on about why killing billions of people is a promising idea, I untied myself. Look at the opt-in numbers. They continue to increase. They're already at eight billion."

More security alarms ring, snapping Drazen out of his trance. He assesses the room, noticing Alyssa has untied herself and is sitting beside Matt. He says, "It's unfortunate I must leave you now, just as we started to understand each other. I will be at a significant disadvantage when you untie Boson and I'm unable to reach Fitz for support. Don't fret, I'll return shortly."

He leaves and locks them in the room.

Matt asks Alyssa, "How are you feeling?"

"Still a little groggy but physically fine. I heard most of the conversation, and it was very disturbing. We need to escape before he gets back with Fitz."

"I agree, but the windows are not an option, as the conference room is over thirty stories up, and the ceiling is higher than we can reach. The conference room is sealed tight as a drum," Matt says, discouraged.

"The doors are digitally locked. Can you use some of your fancy hacking tools and open one of them?"

Behind them, the screen shows a number exceeding nine billion as the date changes from Tuesday to Wednesday. Alyssa asks, "Is this over? Have we already lost?"

"No," Matt reassures her, "the protocol is not automatic. Drazen needs to initiate it with his biometric data, and while he's gone finding Fitz, we need to make sure he can't do it. We need to stop him by modifying the code."

Alyssa asks, "Do you know how to do that?"

"I don't have enough time to figure it out myself, but Drazen and Fitz said something that leads me to believe there's someone who can. I'll open the door, but we need to leave."

"Why?" Alyssa shouts. "The computer access to the Path Program is right here. Why would we leave?"

"Do you trust me?" Matt asks.

"With my life."

"Okay, let's go."

# 52

## THE CUBE

The elevator ride down from the boardroom is quiet. Both Matt and Alyssa try to comprehend what's happening.

As Matt opens the door to the quantum solutions control room, he's happy to see there is no activity.

Alyssa asks, "Where is everyone?"

"They must have been evacuated when the Daedalus attack started."

"Okay, then what are we doing here?"

"Drazen was talking about my father, and he said he hid him right under my feet."

"He's a liar and a sociopath. You can't trust anything he says," Alyssa replies, "and besides, I doubt he was being literal."

"Didn't you see how excited he was? I don't believe his ego would let him lie about this. He wants...no, he needs...to prove he's smarter than all of us. My father's secret is somehow tied to where I work every day, like a sick joke. Let's split up and take a careful look around the office."

"What are we looking for?"

"I don't know."

"Well, that narrows it down," she says, exasperated.

Matt comments, "It's strange being in here when it's completely quiet. Most of the time, there are a dozen conversations and noise from the equipment in the background."

"Yes, the only thing I hear is a recurring clicking sound in this exhaust vent."

Matt pauses. "Yes, I hear it too. It sounds like it's coming from underneath us. I always thought this vent went up and out of the building."

Matt pulls the vent cover off and looks down the shaft. "It looks like it drops a few feet and then turns. It will be tight, but I can fit. I'm going down there."

"Are you crazy? There's an operating fan at the end of the shaft."

"I know. I just need to see where it goes. If it's a dead end, I'll come right back."

Matt shimmies headfirst down the vent and sees the cooling fan vibrating, causing the blade to occasionally strike the casing. On the other side, he can see the outline of another room. *This isn't possible. My office and the lab are the lowest level of the facility. Why wasn't I told there was a room below me?* He kicks the center brace of the fan repeatedly until its casing comes free and falls to the ground.

Alyssa yells, "Are you okay? What is all the noise?"

"I'm fine. Come down here. There's something you need to see."

Alyssa and Matt look around the room. "It's square, like a cube," Alyssa says.

"Exactly. It's a standard engineering and coding configuration with high-end equipment at every station. It looks like it could hold a hundred people, and there's a platform up there where someone could be watching and managing the activities. Let's go up there."

As they climb the ladder to the platform, Alyssa notices a familiar shape on the platform. "It looks like someone is using an old cryogenic chamber as an office desk."

She moves to the front of the desk and screams. "There's someone inside the chamber."

Matt hurries over and stops dead in his tracks. He falls to his knees and begins to cry.

"What's wrong?" Alyssa asks, concerned.

Matt whispers, "That's my father."

Alyssa checks the digital control panel. "The readings are consistent with him being alive."

"How is that possible?" Matt asks.

"These chambers were made to support space travel over vast distances. Theoretically, they can function for dozens of years. This one is in great condition."

"How do you know that? Do you know how to deactivate it...to get him out?" Matt asks.

"The effectiveness of these pods was a key challenge to Gaio when we first met. He showed me numerous prototypes and even trained me to operate one with him inside...to test its functionality. Over time, I learned a lot about how they work. Well, at least how they operated years ago. This model is from roughly the same time period, but they're not identical. I'm rusty, and it will take me some time."

"The only person with the knowledge to shut down the Path Program is inside that chamber, which is why I went looking for him in the cube rather than try to do it myself. We need to get him out."

Alyssa tests different series of steps trying to activate the "revive" function.

At the same time, Matt makes his way around the cube, studying the hardware and related artificial intelligence tools throughout. *It's a unique and innovative way to configure the learning and development protocols. I can use this for...*

Alyssa interrupts. "I think I've figured it out. The only thing left is to push the revive button."

Matt springs up the ladder three rungs at a time. "What are you waiting for? Wake him up!"

"It's not that easy, Matt. If I didn't properly configure the steps, it could kill him, and I won't have that guilt on my shoulders. If you want to proceed, you need to push the revive button."

Matt squeezes his head, trying to make sense of the irony of the situation. *My dad's gambling addiction set in motion events that nearly ruined my life. Now, I have to make the ultimate gambler's decision, and if I'm wrong, I will end his life and likely billions of others.*

Matt's trembling hand presses the button. Thirty minutes crawl by before the door finally swings open. John Boson wakes up, groggy and confused. His eyes land on the blurry outline of Alyssa. "Where am I?" he asks.

"You're in the cube," Matt says from behind the chamber.

John tries to stand, loses his balance, and falls back into the chamber. “I have cryo sickness.”

Matt picks him up and places him in a chair.

John’s vision clears, and he looks at Matt. “Son, I’m sorry.”

Twenty years of pain surge through Matt’s body, immediately replaced by a wave of relief. His arms wrap around his father. “This is going to sound cold, but we don’t have time to reminisce. Drazen is moments away from unleashing death and destruction on billions of people using the Path Program. You’re the only one who can stop him.”

“You found my message.”

“Yes.”

“I put the kill instructions at the end. Why didn’t you use them?”

“Only the first part of the message was intact.”

Alyssa says, “We need to get back to the conference room. Your dad can access the system from there and execute the kill instructions.”

# 53

## THE SHOT

Drazen approaches Fitz at the back security gate. Fitz and his team are engaged in a firefight with an advance team from Daedalus.

Fitz yells to Drazen, "Keep your head down, boss. You're not made for this type of action."

While hiding under a series of crates, he shouts back at Fitz, "Why don't we fall back to a more secure area. Their advance team is progressing toward the loading dock doors and firing at us from all directions."

While Fitz is distracted, a Daedalus team member climbs the crates to get a clear shot at Drazen. Fitz looks up to see what's happening and, as the trigger is pulled, dives in front of Drazen, taking the bullet himself.

Other members of Fitz's team move closer to provide support. Fitz is lying flat next to Drazen. Drazen feels a wetness underneath him and jumps up, screaming, "Did you wet yourself?"

Fitz laughs. "I told you this wasn't for you. It's not piss, boss."

Drazen sees the pool of blood from where he was just sitting. "Are you seriously hurt? Can you move?"

"I'm fine," Fitz responds. "It's a clean entry in the front and exit out my back. These sons of bitches bleed a lot, but I can make it."

Drazen helps Fitz to his feet while Fitz pulls a gel from his vest and applies it to both sides of the wound. He also pulls a small flask from his pocket and takes a long drink. "There you go, good as new until I see the doc."

Fitz screams to his team, "Hold them off as long as possible." He then says to Drazen, "We need to get back to the conference room and start the protocol."

Drazen and Fitz disappear through the loading-dock doors.

# 54

## THE APPROACH

Seventy-five million miles away, the second gravitational wave reaches Icharus 9, causing near-catastrophic system damage. A spark in the equipment causes a fire in the cabin. With the automated fire-management systems down, Commander Aria grabs a contingency extinguisher and puts it out manually. *On a two-hundred-billion-dollar spacecraft, nothing beats this old technology.*

She then checks navigation and comms. Both are dead, entombing her in a rudderless ship. *I have to warn them.*

She realizes the absurdity of this thought. *Even if comms were working, gravitational waves and communication signals both travel at the speed of light. The wave is already gone, so communication is useless.*

She looks out the window toward Earth, knowing the wave is a mere six minutes from reaching it.

The wave barrels through the cosmos, speeding through outer-rim satellites, which crackle and spark as it passes through. It moves farther, getting closer and closer to Earth.

# 55

## A WAVE IN TIME

Matt and Alyssa position John in the corner of the conference room, hiding him from sight in case Fitz and Drazen return. He begins to work, and within a minute, he stops.

"What's wrong?" Matt asks.

"The cryo sickness is making it difficult for me to gather my thoughts. The kill program is complex and will require precise instructions to activate. I can't seem to find my focus."

Alyssa sees Drazen helping Fitz off the elevator. "They're coming," she screams at Matt.

"We'll keep them busy as long as possible while you gain your senses and activate the kill switch. Keep quiet so they don't hear you."

Drazen and Fitz return to the conference room. Drazen helps Fitz into his favorite chair, holding one hand over the hole in his stomach and the other on his pistol.

Drazen comments, "Your friends from Daedalus may

be able to overwhelm our defenses, but they're too late to save the two of you and the other nine billion scum of humanity. All I need is to validate this key with my biomarkers and it starts. People will leave their homes and go to the areas we programmed. Soon after, Farms around the world will begin welcoming the nutrients needed to replenish our oceans and farmlands. It will be impossible to stop."

Alyssa says to Matt, "We need to buy more time. Do you remember when we joined the two-on-two intramural basketball league?"

"Yes, but that is so random."

"Well, it's me on Fitz and you on Drazen. Go cover your man."

Alyssa approaches Fitz. He smiles and puts the pistol back in his pocket. "Be careful. I'm not mortally wounded."

She steps back as he lunges toward her, sidestepping his first advance and pushing him away.

"All you're doing is making me more upset," Fitz says. He then flips a chair at Alyssa, catching her off guard, and uses his strength to pin her in the corner. He grabs her by the neck, choking her.

Matt hears the chair crash against the wall and looks to see Alyssa in trouble. *If I don't stop Drazen, billions of people may die. If I don't stop Fitz, Alyssa dies.* Without hesitation, Matt rushes to her, enflamed with anger. He crashes into Fitz, knocking him away from Alyssa.

Fitz tries to stand straight, but the bullet wound has opened, causing him to hunch over. He lunges forward awkwardly, giving Matt the opportunity to punch him in the stomach.

Fitz collapses and yells, "Who are you to try and save humanity? The wretched people don't even know what's good for them."

"Well, I know they should be given a fair chance and not manipulated into submission. Your plans are at an end," Matt says confidently.

Fitz reaches for his firearm, but Matt stomps on his hand and grabs the gun. In a final effort, Fitz kicks Matt in the groin, causing Matt to accidentally pull the trigger. Fitz drops, lying motionless in a pool of his blood.

Matt rushes to Alyssa.

"I'm fine," she says, "but look at Drazen. His hand is near the key."

Alyssa screams, "Please don't do it!"

"I'll do what I must," Drazen shouts back as he lowers his hand closer.

"You always were second best," a voice from the corner rings through the room.

Drazen stops and grins slightly. "I see they found you. Perfect. One less loose end for me to deal with after I activate the Path Program. I'll let Matt fill you in on how I beat you both, beat Niera, and beat the whole world." He looks down and validates his biometric data.

As Matt lifts the revolver, Drazen flips the switch. "Too late. Tomorrow, the world will wake to a different order, with different rules and rulers able to sustain ourselves for hundreds of years."

Matt and Alyssa embrace. Seconds feel like hours. Terror grips their thoughts. *Will these be the final moments of life for billions? How long before people leave their homes for the Farm? Will humanity be lost forever?*

A look of concern covers their faces, and then the lights and systems shut down. The massive gravity wave penetrates Earth. No human can even sense it, but it's chaos inside GOD's quantum computers. Cages filled with qubits stretch and shrink, allowing the qubits' wave functions to tunnel through the cages. No longer maintained in a single cage, they overlap and destroy most of the higher-level GOD systems. A few moments later, the emergency lighting engages.

Drazen looks at the screen; the number of hosts is zero. "That's not possible. I turned the switch. Billions should be heading to the Farm right now." He checks the quantum diagnostics and sees a massive system failure. The Path Program and the Farm are destroyed.

Drazen looks at John. "What have you done?"

John turns to Matt and says, "I'm sorry. I never engaged the kill switch."

"How then did everything get destroyed?" Drazen demands.

"It happened," Alyssa says. "The second wave passed through Earth. It destroyed everything but saved everyone."

Matt, fueled by a new hatred, squares his shoulders and faces the man who nearly destroyed everyone he loved.

He locks eyes with Drazen. "The devastation unfolding now is not just a technical failure, it's the collapse of a legacy built on arrogance and greed. All your supposed genius, your boundless arrogance, and the insatiable greed of GOD and its puppet masters have been obliterated in an instant by the universe's own natural hand.

The very shortcuts you took, and the fragile quantum cages you rushed into place, have become the wreckage of your ambitions...a testament to the folly of trying to outwit nature itself."

"The world has another chance," Alyssa says as she kisses Matt.

# 56

## THE PURSUIT

Drazen bolts from the room, Matt and Alyssa close behind. He leads them to Niera's office. She lies motionless on her couch, a mind-control collar wrapped around her neck. Drazen clutches a small device in his hand.

"You don't realize what you've committed this world to" he says, his voice cold. I could have saved everyone the pain...the suffering."

"No, you would have taken their very souls from them and created food for an arrogant group of lecherous elites. The world will hear the truth from Niera," Matt shouts back.

Drazen responds, "The world will hear nothing from Niera. I won't let her get away while I wither in some jail." He adjusts the coding on the device and puts his hand on Niera's forehead. "Goodbye," he says.

A gunshot echoes. Blood streaks down Drazen's face as he collapses on the floor. Gaio stands in the doorway, arm extended, gripping a vintage .357 Magnum.

"There's nothing like this old technology," he says, a hint of satisfaction in his voice.

Matt pulls the collar from Niera's neck. Shortly after, she opens her eyes and asks, "What happened?"

Gaio kneels in front of the couch and gently strokes Niera's hair. "It's a long story. Why don't you let my medical team help you and I can fill you in."

Niera looks at Matt. "Did you figure out what happened to our systems?"

"Yes, I did."

"I always believed you would."

# 57

## THE AWAKENING

"So, what happens now?" Alyssa asks.

Matt lets out an exasperated laugh. "I'm sure I have no idea."

"There's going to be so much destruction to recover from, so much confusion, so much anger, and so much to explain," Alyssa says. "What's required is a complete reconstruction of society and its infrastructure."

"Yes, but that's what we've always done. Humanity struggles, fails, adapts, and rebuilds. It's the cycle our species has always used to move forward, with one unifying force driving the inertia, pulling them together."

"Like gravity?" She smiles.

Matt wraps his arms around her. "Something like that."

Alyssa steps back and gives Matt a strange look.

"What's that for?" Matt asks.

"Am I putting this together correctly? You could have stopped Drazen from turning the key, but you chose to save me instead. Nine billion lives on one side of the equation and me on the other. Why?"

"There's no world for me without you. It was an easy decision. Besides, I had a feeling the wave would be here in time to save us."

"You're such a liar, but I like the thought of you tapping into your feelings. What do we do now?" she says, looking into his eyes.

He leans in and kisses her, pulling her deeper into his arms.

Downstairs, Gaio is busy issuing new orders to Gardens around the world.

In the following weeks, billions are freed from bondage and introduced to a new reality. Under Gaio's leadership, the United Nations brings calm and order, using its massive structure to assure safety and food supplies. Governance is returned to sovereign nations that commit to use their technological capabilities to enhance life globally.

# 58

## THE CONTACT LENS

**Six Months Later**

Matt waits patiently near his front door as Alyssa slips on her high-heeled shoes for an afternoon out. Looking in the hallway mirror, she pulls down firmly on the dress, causing it to settle perfectly across her figure.

"What do you think, shorty?" She smiles at Matt, knowing the heels added to her already-above-average height making her an inch taller than he is.

"Good thing I've become so good with my hands. With that dress tight in all the right places, I'll be busy fighting off the guys all night."

Minutes later, on the outskirts of town, Eugene stares at two bottles of beer on the other side of the table. Before anyone has time to comment, Matt picks them up and passes one to Alyssa as he leads a "cheers" to all of his team.

• • •

Back at GOD headquarters, a board meeting is wrapping up. Niera is agitated despite receiving praise for her renewed leadership and support of the world's needs.

In her private office, she looks into a bathroom mirror, rubbing her eyes. A contact lens pops out, landing on the counter.

Niera's head begins to twitch. She sees one brown pupil and one shimmering blue one reflecting back at her.

She slams her fist into the mirror as "not in control, not in control, not in control" echoes in the bathroom.

# INSPIRATION

The inspiration for this novel came from many long conversations with my friend Bill Lee before he passed. We agreed strongly that there was a direct relationship between the integration of advanced technology in human lives and the deteriorating human condition. We also believed the collective human spirit would rise above the elite's wish to bring us to our knees and that the cure for the malady of a suffocating, interconnected world was to get back to nature, community, and spiritual reality.

# ACKNOWLEDGMENTS

Thank you to my wife Jennifer for her support, and belief in me throughout this project. She understood I was a fish out of water and encouraged me to keep going every step of the way. Thank you to Alex Bach for your coaching and story advice and to Alana Lytle for your inspiration and great insights. A huge thanks to my editor, Audra Gerber for being excited about the book and providing numerous ideas to make it better. Also, thank you to the many family and friends for reading early and your positivity.

**MIKE BRITTON** lives in Naperville, Illinois, with his wife, Jennifer. He has three children and several grandkids. He is a successful business entrepreneur with a deep interest in physics, humanity, and societal trends.

www.ingramcontent.com/pod-product-compliance
Lightning Source LLC
LaVergne TN
LVHW090555110826
845146LV00001B/133

* 9 7 9 8 9 9 4 7 4 4 1 0 9 *